Of Love and Corn Dogs

By
Parker Williams

COPYRIGHT

ACKNOWLEDGEMENTS

The author acknowledges the trademarked status and trademark owners of the following trademarks mentioned in this work of fiction:

Corvette (Stingray): General Motors, LLC
Golden Chicken: Four Brothers, Inc.
Kendall-Jackson merlot: Jackson Family Wines, Inc.
Mac: Apple, Inc.
Macallan M: The Macallan Distillers Limited.
McDonald's: McDonald's Corporation
MIT: Massachusetts Institute of Technology Corporation
NASDAQ: NASDAQ, Inc.
Prada: Prada S.A.
The Godfather: Paramount Pictures Corporation

Contents

OF LOVE AND CORN DOGS

With more money than he could spend in ten lifetimes, Darwin Kincade still couldn't keep death from stealing his lover. A little older and a whole lot wiser, flirting with his twice-a-week waiter is the perfect no-risk substitute for a real relationship. Until the night his routine is upended by the restaurant's newest employee.

Ricky Donnelly loves people. While being a server isn't his dream, he's good at it. When a grumpy man is seated in his station, Ricky sees there's more to him than he lets on, and when the man relaxes, he's actually sweet.

As the two men bond over a discussion about corn dogs—something Darwin's never heard of—he realizes how much he's missed out on in his life. He vows to open himself to new experiences—including, perhaps, a chance at finding love again.

Not wanting anything to muddy their blooming relationship, Darwin hides part of himself from Ricky. He likes the look in Ricky's eyes, unclouded by Darwin's notoriety. Unfortunately, the truth can never stay hidden, and when it comes out, Darwin may lose any hope of holding onto the future they've begun to build.

CHAPTER ONE

Darwin sat at his usual table and scanned the restaurant, anxious to see Roy, his favorite server. From the soft lighting of the candelabras that dotted the walls and the gleaming hardwood bar to the deep, rich brown carpeting, everything about Asiago screamed class. As the only five-star restaurant in the area, everything had to be the best. But Roy outshone all the glitz of the dining room. While Darwin knew Roy saw him as a customer, he secretly hoped that one day the waiter might realize he hadn't been coming for the food all these months.

He frowned when the young man who approached the table looked nothing like the raven-haired beauty Darwin had grown accustomed to seeing twice a week for the last six months. He tried to school his features to hide his disappointment, not wanting to hurt the slender blond with the wide smile who drew near.

"Good evening, Mr. Kincade. My name is Richard, and I'll be your server for this evening. Would you like to start with a drink?"

"Where's Roy?" Darwin growled. His cheeks heated when Richard stepped back, looking every bit the kicked puppy. Darwin winced. He knew better than to snap at people. He scratched his cheek before he glanced up. "I'm sorry. It's been a long day. Please forgive me. I assume Roy isn't working tonight?"

"Roy quit a couple days ago," came the hesitant answer.

Darwin's gut clenched. He'd been coming to Asiago simply for Roy. Truthfully, the merely palatable food hadn't been a drawing point. Seeing Roy had become the highlight of his week, and now he was gone.

"Did he say where he was going?" A hint of whine escaped, but goddamn it, he'd been in lust with Roy.

"He and his wife moved to be closer to her parents."

Nausea rolled through Darwin. He hadn't even considered Roy might not have been gay. Such a fool he was.

"Would you like that drink?" Richard asked hesitantly.

Darwin knew Asiago was one of the few places in the United States that had the drink he loved most. "Yes, please. A shot of Macallan M. Neat."

Richard gasped and then covered his mouth. "Sir, that costs—"

"I damn well know the cost," he snapped. "Bring me my drink."

Once more Darwin's anger had gotten the better of him. Green eyes shimmered in the dim lighting, and Darwin worried the young man might break into tears.

"Again, please accept my apologies. It's been a rough day, and I should probably just go home." He reached over and grabbed his briefcase, ready to stand, when Richard held out a hand and graced Darwin with a genuine and disarming smile.

"No, please. Stay. Let me get you that drink, okay? I'll let you know the dinner special when I come back. My grandma always said any day can be made better with a good meal." Richard hurried off in the direction of the bar without waiting for a reply.

Darwin fumed at his lack of self-control. Not only had he made a fool of himself tonight, but he'd also hurt the feelings of someone he didn't know. Though Richard would be right to refuse service to Darwin, he'd run to get a drink. As much as he wanted to believe the attentive attitude came down to getting a decent tip, Richard seemed too genuine for that. Darwin sighed and put his briefcase back on the leather seat. His mother would be so disappointed in him.

A crystal glass thunked against the table, startling Darwin. The amber liquid rippled gently. Darwin picked it up and gazed into the glass. He'd thought about downing it in one go, relishing the burn that would inevitably follow, but he hated losing control. He took a deep, steadying breath.

"Richard—"

"Ricky."

"Excuse me?"

"Most people call me Ricky. You can, if you want."

Darwin smiled at him, hoping to convey his contrition. "Ricky, then. I'm very sorry. I'm out of sorts, and it's not fair to you that I'm being so…" Darwin looked for just the right word.

"Antagonistic?"

Darwin reared back in his seat and looked at the young man, who was now giving him a cheeky grin. He couldn't help but be put at ease by the gentle teasing. "Okay, we'll go with that."

"I'm sorry I'm not Roy," Ricky told him. "I'd only met him when I got hired here. He was a great waiter, and I doubt I can fill his shoes. If you prefer, I'll find you someone else."

"No, I think you'll do just fine. Tell me about the dinner special."

This time Ricky's smile didn't quite reach his eyes. "Tonight we have a truffle-braised tenderloin served with whipped dauphinoise potatoes and honey-glazed carrots." In fact, as he recited the special, it became obvious the whole shtick had been practiced to death.

Darwin grinned. His turn to do a little teasing. "And what did you think of it?"

"Excuse me?" Ricky asked, obviously not expecting the question.

Darwin tapped his index finger on the table, feigning irritation. The adorable look of consternation on Ricky's face amused him. "I assume you tried it, so what did you think?"

Ricky bit the corner of one lip, then glanced around, before he leaned forward and whispered, "Honestly? I thought it was pretentious. Give me a corn dog any day."

Darwin burst out laughing, which drew unhappy stares from the patrons at nearby tables. He didn't care. "What's a corn dog?"

"It's a… Well, it's…" Ricky blinked a couple of times. "You really don't know what a corn dog is? Seriously?"

"Well…no. I don't know that I've ever had one. Do you think they can make me one here?"

Ricky snorted. "Chef Michael thinks corn dogs aren't even real food. He claims he wouldn't feed them to his Pekingese. So, no, you definitely won't find corn dogs here."

Darwin had to admit, he'd never really had a taste for Asiago's cuisine. And Ricky's certainty that a corn dog would be better had intrigued him. "Then can you tell me where to find your favorite one?"

"The best ones in town are at the mini-putt course over on Klein."

"Mini-putt?"

Ricky shook his head. "You're kidding, right? How do you not know these things?"

Darwin sat back and grinned. Ricky had no idea who Darwin was, and he found the anonymity oddly refreshing. He leaned forward and put his chin on the palm of his hand. "I lead a sheltered life, apparently. So, if I want a corn dog, I need to go to the mini-putt place." Ricky gave a slight nod, and Darwin chuckled. "Okay, I'll do that."

He stood, picked up his briefcase and began to move toward the door when the manager, Louisa, rushed to his table. She scowled at Ricky, which had Darwin's teeth grinding.

"Mr. Kincade, is something wrong?" she asked quietly, obviously not wanting the other patrons to witness the discussion.

"No, everything is perfect. I like this young man," he said, waving a hand toward Ricky. "He's refreshing."

The condescending look Louisa gave Ricky told him she didn't agree. "If he's done anything to upset you—"

"Wait. Why would you think he upset me? If anything, I was the responsible party. Ricky did nothing wrong at all. He talked me into a nice drink, and that's all I needed for tonight." He turned to Ricky. "I'll stop at the bar to pay for the drink. Thank you for a most entertaining evening."

He reached into his wallet and peeled off two one-hundred-dollar bills, which he tossed on the table. "For your time and trouble," he said to Ricky, then started for the door again. He turned and noted Louisa's body language—tense, with her gaze fixed on Ricky, who appeared nervous, and that didn't sit well with Darwin at all.

"I'm coming back Monday. Please reserve me a table, and note that I want Ricky as my server."

If she'd had a mouthful of water, she'd have spit it everywhere. She jabbed a finger in Ricky's direction. "You want...him?"

Darwin narrowed his gaze. The manager's attitude, coupled with the helpless expression on Ricky's face had him feeling protective. "Yes. Is there a problem with that?"

She moved forward and put a hand on his back as she guided him to the door. Darwin forced himself to remain calm. He didn't like people touching him without his permission, and this woman had already gotten his dander up.

"Well," she said slowly. "Ricky is on probation. He hasn't exactly been working out. He's slow and has been argumentative with customers."

"Yet he was perfect with me. Perhaps the issue was the customers and not the server. Maybe you should consider that. I expect him to be here Monday. If he's not..."

Darwin left the threat unvoiced. Unlike Ricky, Louisa knew who he was and what he could do if he wanted. He left the woman standing there, huffing like a wild beast, as he stepped out of the restaurant into the cool Chicago night. He gazed wistfully back at the front of the restaurant while he called his driver. Roy was gone, but...Ricky seemed as though he'd be very interesting, too.

Roy had never engaged Darwin in conversation. He'd never been even remotely friendly. The only thing he really had going for him were his looks. Ricky had looks, too, but he also had panache.

Darwin looked forward to seeing him again.

The long, sleek limo pulled up a few moments later. A tall, slender man stepped out, dressed in a black suit and hat, and began to round the car. He frowned, no doubt wondering why Darwin had called him already.

"That was fast, Dare."

Darwin grinned at his oldest friend. "They didn't have what I wanted for dinner tonight. The new waiter suggested something, and I find I really want to try it."

He'd been friends with Henley since they were kids, and he rarely frazzled the man. So, Henley's puzzled expression delighted Darwin. He wondered what he'd say when he told him where they were going. Henley opened the back door to the limousine, then closed it after Darwin slid in. He returned to the driver's side and started the car.

"Okay, where to?"

"We're going to the mini-putt course on Klein for a corn dog."

At that moment, Darwin wished he'd had his phone out to take a picture. He'd frame the shot and hang it in the house so everyone could see Henley looking as though his jaw had unhinged and was now resting atop his polished shoes.

Yes, Ricky could be an inspiration to me.

"This is a corn dog?" Darwin asked, biting into the savory breading.

"Dude, I cannot believe you've never had a corn dog," Henley said through a mouthful of his own. "My mom used to give them to us every Friday along with cheese fries."

Darwin snorted. "Yes, well, you know my parents would have gone into meltdown if their son had ever touched something greasy."

"And delicious, don't forget that part."

Darwin had to admit, the batter-dipped frankfurter was very tasty. He agreed with Ricky—the corn dogs were a damn sight better than the offered special at Asiago. He reached out and took another french fry, slathered it with ketchup, and popped it into his mouth.

"How did you never tell me about these things?"

"Mom told me your parents might have sacked her if she polluted you with our common ways." Henley shrugged, and he stuffed his mouth full of fries, then grinned, showing off his cheesy smile.

Darwin wanted to protest, but Henley spoke the truth. His parents took great care of their employees, but staff was never meant to be family or friends. They firmly believed in keeping Darwin away from them unless absolutely necessary. Still, he and Henley had snuck away most nights, hiding out in one of the unused rooms of the mansion.

He'd shared his secrets with Henley. Henley had listened when Darwin spoke hesitantly about his crush on his tutor. And Henley had been the person with whom Darwin had shared his first kiss. His anxiety during the worst board meeting after taking over the company paled in comparison to the terror of that moment when their lips met. So many thoughts had gone through Darwin's head in that instant—how cool Henley's lips were as they brushed against his, how he'd known Henley had sucked on a mint, judging by the flavor, and how he'd wished the kiss had been with the tutor instead of Henley, because there had been no emotion there for either of them.

"Do you remember our kiss?" Darwin asked, glancing toward his friend.

Henley rolled his eyes. "You never forget your first kiss. Even if the person you kissed had a serious case of fish lips going on."

Darwin gasped and covered his heart with his hand. "I so did not."

"You're such a drama queen." Henley bit into his corn dog then swallowed hard. "All I can say is I hope you've gotten better at it. If you'd kissed like that when you were with Dean— Oh, shit. Dare, I'm sorry."

An icy fist gripped Darwin's heart. God, he missed Dean.

"It's okay," he whispered.

"No, it's not. I shouldn't have said it."

Darwin shrugged. "It's been six years." Six years, seven months, and twelve days since Darwin had lost the only man he'd ever really loved. He'd watched as Dean had wasted away, becoming thinner, paler. Darwin had known all the money in the world couldn't save him from the cancer that consumed him.

"I know. But I also know there hasn't been anyone since then. Or am I mistaken?"

"Please. You'd be the first person I'd tell." He smiled when Henley's cheeks pinked.

"I appreciate that."

They finished their meal in silence, then Henley threw away the trash, and returned the tray to the stack. "You know," he started, "we *could* continue your education on what good food is."

Mischief danced in Henley's eyes, and Darwin couldn't help but be intrigued.

"Oh, do tell?"

"Wait here. I'll be right back."

Darwin chuckled. "Since you have the keys to the limo, I think I'm pretty well stuck until you're ready."

Henley gave his trademark cheeky grin, then headed back into the small restaurant attached to the mini-putts course. When he returned, he carried two very large paper cups with clear plastic domes on them. Inside was a thick concoction, topped with whipped cream and chocolate shavings. He placed one in front of Darwin, then pulled the lid off his own.

"You'll need to take the top off," Henley explained. "The shakes are way too rich to use a straw."

Then Henley tilted it back and began chugging down the frosty beverage. Darwin followed his example, lifting the cup to his lips. The smell of fruit had nothing on the flavors bursting on his tongue. Tart berries and sweet ice cream, plus the richness of the topping, had Darwin moaning.

"Good, right? This is a raspberry nebula shake. Those bits in there are chocolate chips."

Fuck. Darwin had found his new favorite dessert. His whole life had been sliced melons or some other thing the staff served. His mother had insisted on proper nutrition and thought that sweet things were the devil's work. Once, he'd seen Henley eating a chocolate bar and begged for a bite. His friend had hesitated, then made Darwin promise not to tell. After he'd given his word, Henley had broken off a small piece and handed it over. It had been indescribably delicious, and Darwin had tried not to chew, to let it melt in his mouth so he'd be able to enjoy it as long as possible. He regretted that he'd missed out on things like this during his childhood, and that those habits had carried on into adulthood.

"Welcome to my world, Dare," Henley said, tipping the cup toward Darwin. "It's nice of you to visit."

Darwin never really thought of the divide that existed between him and Henley. In Darwin's mind, they were equals. But the comment he'd just made reminded Darwin that he didn't belong in this kind of place, eating corn dogs and drinking shakes. But, damn it, he refused to feel guilty about finally enjoying something.

"I want to play mini-putts," he said emphatically.

"You have that meeting at eight with Kent and his board, remember?"

A groan escaped Darwin's lips. He'd forgotten the discussion his brother had scheduled to talk about Darwin taking over his company, which had gone deep into the red. The only way to avoid foreclosure would be for new management, the kind with deep pockets, to step in and bail them out. Almost since birth, Darwin had been schooled on the importance of business, how it had to come before everything else.

He'd taken that lesson to heart every day of his life, including the one time he shouldn't have. Dean had been so sick, but Darwin had been scheduled to meet with foreign investors who were only in the States for a week. That would be the only opportunity he had to meet with them. Darwin had wanted to cancel, but Dean had urged him to go. He'd protested, and Dean had reminded him how important that deal was, not only to Kincade International, but also to the employees who worked there. So Darwin had gone. They'd wined and dined him, then signed the agreement. He'd returned home flush with pride at sealing the deal. That had lasted until he spotted the ambulance in the driveway, loading a gurney with Dean on it into the back. Darwin had rushed over and clutched his lover's hand.

Dean had reached up to pull the oxygen mask off, despite the paramedic saying it needed to stay in place.

"How...did...it...go?" he'd gasped out.

"We got everything we wanted."

Dean had reached out a trembling hand and stroked Darwin's face. "I knew you could."

Then his hand had fallen away, and the paramedics had called the police officer over to take Darwin so they could work on Dean. His lover had died on the trip to the hospital, Darwin never getting the opportunity to tell him how sorry he was for leaving him alone. Never getting the chance to tell him he wanted to marry him. The man was his husband in everything but name, and now he could never be more.

Tonight he'd be self-indulgent.

"I want to play mini-putts," he repeated. He pulled out his phone and speed-dialed his assistant.

"Heather, I want you to call my brother and reschedule the meeting. It won't be taking place tonight after all."

"But, Mr. Kincade, it's all been arranged." Heather sounded flustered, which was unusual for her. She could face a horde of reporters and never bat an eye.

"Then rearrange it. Tell him something came up at the last moment, and I'm unable to attend."

She answered in her usual business-like tone, clipped and efficient. "Yes, sir. I'll take care of it right away. Is there anything else I can do for you?"

Darwin thought for a moment before he answered. "Yes. I'd like a reservation at Asiago on Monday. Make sure you request Ricky as my server. Tell the manager I want no one else, and that Ricky is to serve only me. I don't want him waiting on other tables while I'm there. Let her know we'll pay for his time, so she won't have to worry about that." Then an idea came to Darwin. "And tell her I want corn dogs."

"You want… I'm sorry, I think we may have a bad connection. Did you say you wanted corn dogs?"

"I did. And let them know I want corn dogs, cheese fries, and a raspberry nebula shake."

"At Asiago? You know they're not likely to have that, right?"

"Make sure you tell Louisa it's for me, and she can find everything she needs at the mini-putts place on Klein Street. I'm sure she'll make arrangements." Darwin grinned. He wished he could see the snooty restaurant manager's face when Heather relayed his orders. She should know better than to be rude to her staff. Especially Ricky, who'd been absolutely perfect as far as Darwin was concerned.

"And how many people shall I make the reservation for?"

"Just me, but I want enough food for two people."

He thought he heard Henley whispering something in the background, but he chose to ignore his friend.

"Yes, sir. I'll take care of it."

"I know you will, Heather. And thank you. I really appreciate this."

Her voice softened. "You know all of us are happy to do what you ask."

It was true. Darwin's parents had always treated their workers very well. They'd instituted the first employer sponsored, on premise daycare center in the state, leave was available after the birth of a child for both mothers and fathers, they received well above average salaries for their positions, and the turnover rate was practically nil.

"I know," Darwin answered. And he did. He never took them for granted. Without his staff, he had no company to run. "Please send my regrets to my brother. If you can, reschedule him for early next week. Just not on Monday, okay?"

"Understood, sir. I hope your business goes well."

He turned as Henley stepped out of the restaurant, two putters in his hand, and a wide smile on his face.

"I think it's going to be a great night."

CHAPTER TWO

Ricky glanced at his watch again. The reservation had been made for seven thirty, and it had just turned eight. Perhaps Mr. Kincade had gotten tied up with something and couldn't make it. When Louisa told him that he'd be working the private party, he had been stunned. Then when she tipped her glasses down and glared at him, reminding him that he should already be out the door, he lowered his head. He thought he'd been doing a good job, but it had become obvious he wasn't Roy, and the staff had told him that the young man had been Louisa's favorite.

"Where is he?" Louisa grumbled.

"I don't know," Ricky answered, then flinched when she glared at him.

"Whatever you did to get in his good graces, it won't keep you on the payroll. You'll mess up and he'll complain, then you'll be out the door."

Sweat trickled down Ricky's arms, tickling the fine hair there. If he had guts, he'd walk out and let her explain to Mr. Kincade why the waiter he'd requested wasn't there. But school wasn't cheap. He needed this job, and if it meant he had to take her abuse, then so be it.

"Louisa, Mr. Kincade just walked through the door," the busboy whispered.

She turned and gave Ricky the death stare he'd seen a dozen times, before she rushed to greet Mr. Kincade.

"Thank you for coming," she gushed as they approached Ricky's station. She put her hand on his back, until Mr. Kincade turned to

19

glare at her. She swept her hand toward Ricky. "Your private room is ready, as is your server."

The man's smile took Ricky's breath away. The day he'd first seen the man seated in his station, Ricky had been so nervous he prayed he wouldn't make a fool of himself. Even though that night started out bad, it quickly got better when Mr. Kincade relaxed enough to show he could be a little fun.

Of course, *that* only lasted until he'd walked out the door. Then Louisa had been angrier than he'd ever seen her. She'd muttered something about snobs, then stormed into her office and slammed the door, much to the chagrin of the staff. Still, it felt good to know something could ruffle her feathers.

"My apologies for being late," Mr. Kincade said. "I had something I had to attend to, and it couldn't wait."

"Nonsense," Louisa purred. "We're only too happy to hold a table for you."

She escorted him to the room and pulled out his chair. When he glanced at Ricky and gave him a sly wink, Ricky's pulse sped up.

"As you requested, Richard will be your server this evening. Should you require anything, please don't hesitate to ask me. Oh, and we were able to accommodate your dinner request tonight as well."

Her lip curled, and Ricky saw she'd been digging her nails into her palm to keep from snapping. When she'd told Ricky that Mr. Kincade had very special requests for the evening, he could barely contain his curiosity.

After Louisa walked out the door, Ricky stepped up to the table.

"Good evening, Mr. Kincade. How are you tonight?"

"Would it be out of line if I asked you to call me Darwin?"

Ricky scrunched his brow. "I'm...not sure Louisa would approve."

"Oh, I'm very certain she doesn't approve of many things. And, so you know, I really don't care."

Ricky couldn't help the chuckle that bubbled out of him. Mr. Kincade—Darwin—had to be the only person he'd ever seen get the best of Louisa. He knew good and well she'd take it out on him after the meal, but for the moment, he intended to enjoy it.

"Very well, Mr....Darwin, I've been told that you have a special order waiting in the kitchen. Are you ready to dine?"

Darwin chuckled and clapped his hands. "Oh, very much. Let's get this show on the road."

Ricky grinned. Darwin's attitude seemed so different from the last time he'd been at the restaurant, his joy infectious. "I'll be back in a couple of minutes."

"I look forward to it," Darwin replied, his cheeky expression growing into a bright smile.

When Ricky entered the kitchen, he noticed a scent he'd never encountered at Asiago before. The aroma tickled his nose and caused his stomach to growl.

"Donnelly," Chef Michael called out, "get this...food out of my kitchen."

Ricky approached the line to pick up the cloth-covered tray the food runner had put together for him, but when he went to remove it, the chef slammed a spoon down.

"Don't lift that cover," the chef snapped. "My instructions were very explicit. You're to take the food to Mr. Kincade, but not to check it until you're in the room with him."

"But what if something's wrong?" Ricky asked, then took a step back when the prickly chef glared at him.

"Are you saying something might be wrong with my food?"

"Well, no, but—"

"Then what are you saying?" he demanded, leaning forward with his big, beefy hands splayed out on the counter. "Spit it out."

Not wanting to confront the chef, Ricky looked down at the tray. "Louisa told me that everything for Mr. Kincade had to be perfect. She's looking for an excuse to can me, so if I mess up, she'll put me out." He glanced up, hoping Michael would understand.

The chef's expression softened a touch. "Ricky, if Louisa has a problem, she can come and talk to me. These were Mr. Kincade's instructions, so she doesn't have a pot to piss in."

Despite Michael's attitude, he never hesitated to stand up for his kitchen staff when Louisa stormed through on the warpath. If he gave his word that everything would be okay, Ricky believed him. He nodded at the chef, then hefted the tray up onto his shoulder, before he darted through the dining room, and up the stairs to the private suite where Mr. Kincade waited.

"Oh, good. I'm glad you're back," Mr. Kincade called out when he entered the room. "Have a seat."

What?

"What? Mr. Kincade—" Ricky protested, as he put the tray down on the stand next to the table.

"Darwin," Mr. Kincade reminded him, a sly grin playing on his lips.

"Darwin... I can't sit down. If Louisa finds me—"

"Your entire service is devoted strictly to me tonight. Louisa is aware of this. So if I want you to sit, then she has nothing to say about it. Of course, if you'd prefer not to, I can understand."

"Well, no, but—"

"Then sit."

Ricky crossed his arms and glared at Darwin. "You're used to getting your way, aren't you?"

Darwin nodded. "Of course. Sit down before the food gets cold."

As Ricky pulled out the chair, Darwin moved over to the tray and removed the cloth. The metal clanged when he tipped the cover of the serving plates slightly, then he chuckled. "Perfect," he said.

He turned around and pinned Ricky with a stare. "Okay, so I was very rude to you last week when I was here, right?"

"I don't know that I'd say you were rude..." Ricky started, then trailed off, somewhat embarrassed at being reminded about his own behavior that day. But it had been so much fun to play with Darwin, who'd loosened up when he finally calmed down about Roy leaving.

"What was the word you used? Oh, yes, antagonistic. And I was. It had been one surprise after another, and if there is one thing I can't abide, it's being surprised. I took it out on you, and that wasn't fair. So I want to take this opportunity to make it up to you."

"That's really not—"

Darwin placed two plates on the table in front of Ricky, then turned and picked up two cups that he added to the settings. Ricky stared at the table, then up at Darwin.

"What's—"

"And you said the chef wouldn't make corn dogs. Shows how much you know."

"You've got this really bad habit of interrupting, you know that?" Ricky said with a frown.

Darwin gave the most infuriating smirk. "Sorry. When I'm in a meeting, it's usually necessary for me to speak up in order to be heard over the noise. I'll try not to make a habit of it."

The grin told him Darwin really wasn't sorry, and Ricky didn't care. It added another dimension to the man's idiosyncrasies. He wanted to say something, but then he looked at the plates again.

"Wait. This isn't something he cooked. This is from the mini-putts place, right?"

Darwin shrugged. "They brought the stuff from there, but made them here in the kitchen. I believe the chef said he'd cook them over his dead body. I'm sorry for your loss," Darwin said with a wink.

The snort came out before Ricky could rein it in. "I take it you liked them?"

Darwin took a seat across from Ricky and smiled. "I did. Thank you for suggesting it. My friend Henley said we needed the shakes, too."

"I...thank you. This is one of the nicest things anyone has ever done for me. You should be antagonistic more often."

The warm, rich laugh Ricky received wrapped around him like a caress. For a minute, he forgot why they were there. He picked up his first corn dog and dipped it in the cheese sauce that the chef had served with it. He closed his eyes and moaned slightly.

"Oh, that's so good. I've missed these."

Darwin cocked his head. "Why?"

"Oh, um...I'm budgeting my money so I can pay off my school loans before I die." He laughed, and took another bite. "Damn, those are good," he said with a sigh and closed his eyes as he chewed.

He couldn't believe Darwin had done this. Ricky hadn't been able to afford his favorite food for a while, and he wanted to relish it. He opened his eyes to Darwin staring at him, a smirk plastered on his face.

"What? Did I drip cheese sauce on me or something?"

"Hmm? Oh, no. Nothing like that. I just like the fact you're enjoying the food."

Feeling his cheeks heat, Ricky dropped his gaze to his plate and muttered, "Sorry."

"Why? I thought it was nice."

In an effort to keep from embarrassing himself further, Ricky reached out for his shake cup, and, of course, knocked it over. The light purple liquid oozed out onto the table and began moving toward the edge.

"Oh, damn. I'm sorry, I... Shit. Let me get something to clean it up."

Ricky ran to the side station and grabbed some serving towels, which he used to try to mop up the mess. When Darwin reached out an arm and dropped it onto the table to impede the flow, Ricky cringed. He didn't know clothes, but with the way Darwin's black suit hugged his physique, it had to have been tailor-made for him.

"Don't. You'll ruin your suit."

Darwin shrugged. "I have another."

Ricky mopped up the mess as best he could, creating a pile of cloths that were soaked with the remnants of his shake. There'd be no hiding this, not that he would. He believed in taking responsibility when he'd been wrong, and this one would be a doozy.

"Ah, well," he said on a sigh, "it wasn't the most glamorous job in the world. I guess I'll have to see if I can find something else."

"What? Why?"

***

The liquid absorbed by Darwin's sleeve had soaked through to his skin and chilled his arm, but that didn't seem as important as the look on Ricky's face. Darwin hadn't kept the position he had inherited without having ample business acumen. He watched people, read their body language, knew when they handed him a line. Ricky's expression spoke of disappointment tinged with sadness, but also of sincerity.

"I'm not Louisa's favorite," he explained as he removed the soiled linen from the table and put it onto the empty serving tray. "I shouldn't be telling you this, but what the hell. It's not like it will matter in an hour anyway. Not long after I took Roy's position, she started to take great joy in letting me know every single thing I did wrong. He wiped up more of the shake, then glanced over to meet Darwin's gaze. "My first day of training, she hovered constantly, and let me know whenever I put a salad fork a millimeter out of place. Don't get me wrong, I do understand. Asiago has a reputation, and as the manager, she needs to maintain certain standards, but sometimes I think she just hates me."

Though Darwin hadn't gone there with any plan other than his apology to Ricky, he found himself studying the man—the gentle curves of his face, the depth of color in his eyes, the radiant smile. Plus, he had an amazing attitude. He'd settled Darwin's discontent during his last visit, despite Darwin's boorish behavior, and Ricky had apologized for not being Roy merely because of his customer's disappointment.

"She's not going to fire you," Darwin promised. "We simply had an accident. I'll pay for the dry-cleaning if it makes it better."

Ricky folded the tablecloth back, the stain spreading over the snowy white linen. "Nah, it was my clumsiness, so I'll let her know. But, before I go, let's eat."

The smile that Ricky had been showing since Darwin arrived had dimmed, and he could clearly see the pain in his eyes.

"Ricky, I—"

"Eat your food. Let's not waste a perfectly good meal worrying about what might happen. If she fires me, then she does. You're spending good money here to wine and dine. The least we can do is make sure the food doesn't go to waste." Ricky bit into one of the corn dogs. "Damn, these are good."

With a heavy heart, Darwin poured some ketchup onto his plate and swirled his own dog around in the red puddle. He'd wanted to do something nice for Ricky, to make up for the absolute bastard he'd been the previous week. He'd thought a good dinner, comprised of food Ricky would enjoy, would go a long way toward soothing any remaining hurt feelings. Instead, he'd put the young man's job in jeopardy.

Thoughts collided in Darwin's head. He could offer to pay for Ricky's schooling. It's not like he'd miss the money. But he didn't want to add an insult to the list of his faux pas. Plus, Ricky didn't seem to know who Darwin was, and Darwin found that liberating. Too often in his life, people would react like Louisa, doing as he wanted because he had money. He'd watched his father remind people of who he was on occasion to curry favor, and it had always embarrassed Darwin so much he'd gladly have dug a hole and crawled in.

"Can you excuse me?" Darwin asked. "I'm going to visit the washroom."

Ricky looked up and gave a watery smile. "Sure. I'm not going anywhere." He reached across the table and snagged one of Darwin's fries. "But don't blame me if your plate is empty when you get back."

He walked down the three steps to the dining room floor and made a beeline toward the hostess stand. As much as he hated the idea of behaving like his father, he simply couldn't let Louisa fire Ricky for something so petty.

"Good evening, Mr. Kincade, how may I help you?" the hostess asked.

Darwin opened his mouth to speak when a hand came to rest on his arm. "He's looking for the bathroom," Ricky told her. "I should have just shown him where it was to start with."

He dragged Darwin away from the desk and marched him toward the bathroom.

"Here you are, sir. The bathroom is right through that door." Then quietly he growled, "Leave it alone, Darwin. Whatever happens happens. It's not for you to try to fix. Okay?"

Ricky's tone showed he would brook no argument. It struck Darwin how much of a marked difference there was between Ricky and Roy. Roy had been professional but cold in his interactions. In fact, Darwin couldn't recall ever seeing a genuine smile on the man's face. Ricky, on the other hand, exuded charm and friendliness.

"I know what it is," Darwin said, his attention still locked on Louisa's office.

"What's that?"

"Why you're not Louisa's favorite. She likes drones. You told me Roy was a good waiter, and that's true. Efficient to a fault. But he had no real personality, at least not on the job. That's what she wants. Asiago is a beautiful place, but it's cold and sterile. You've got warmth and a playful attitude. I don't think it's welcome at a place like this."

Ricky furrowed his brow. "I never thought about it like that. I tried to be the server Louisa wanted, but I never got it right. It's not in my nature to stop being who I am when I walk in here. I like people, and I want them to have a good time. Maybe I play a little too much."

"Well, I'm glad you do. You made my day when I was here last week. After several meetings and talking to prospective clients, I wanted to let my hair down and relax. But Roy never gave me that.

He had always been courteous, but we never had a conversation beyond how much I enjoyed the food."

"But you wanted him to say more, didn't you?"

Darwin shot his gaze to Ricky's face.

"I figured you liked him. He was pretty easy on the eyes, so it shows you have good taste."

"You're right. I did like looking at him, but even if he had been gay, I doubt it would have moved beyond that. I never really gave it too much thought, but Roy had been a guilty pleasure. Stealing glances while he wasn't looking. It hurt a little when you told me he'd moved, but if I'm honest, I don't think I've given him more than a passing thought until now."

Ricky looked over Darwin's shoulder. "And there she is. I suppose I ought to go face the music. I know the night didn't go like you wanted, and I'm very sorry about that, but what you did? I can't thank you enough for it."

Ricky held out his hand and Darwin reached for it. A warm hand and a firm grip. A lump formed in Darwin's throat. Ricky didn't deserve to lose his job. Darwin wanted to come back to Asiago and get to know him better. He needed…more.

"If I get fired, you need to know how much of a pleasure it was serving you."

When Ricky turned away, Darwin fought the temptation to call after him. The expression on Louisa's face as Ricky talked with her spoke volumes. Ricky wasn't meant for a place like this. He didn't deserve to become like Roy.

Louisa's gaze narrowed, and she clutched Ricky's arm and dragged him toward the office. Darwin turned away and took a deep breath. He pulled out his phone and dialed Henley.

"Are you ready, Dare?" his friend asked, the volume on the stereo lowering as he spoke.

"She's going to fire him," Darwin replied. "We had an accident, and it's going to cost Ricky his job."

"She can't do that," Henley protested.

"She's been looking for an excuse," Darwin explained. "I think this qualifies, especially since he's on probation."

"So what are you going to do? I'd march in there and set her straight."

It wasn't as if the thought hadn't crossed his mind. "Ricky wouldn't appreciate it. He's very independent and more than a little stubborn, I think."

"Leave it to you to pick the difficult ones. You have to do something. You can't just let him lose his job."

Darwin stepped closer to the hostess stand as a man entered the washroom. "I don't see where I have a choice. He asked me not to interfere."

"I don't like this," Henley snapped. "From what you say, he's a decent guy. Why is she being so hard-assed about it?"

"The *why* doesn't matter. The *what am I going to do* does." Darwin seldom lost control, but right then the thought that Ricky would lose his job, and all because of something Darwin had done, made him anxious.

"You could always buy the restaurant," Henley said, then chuckled.

"This isn't funny," Darwin growled.

"I know. I'm sorry. Look, if he doesn't want you to do anything, then I don't think you should. He's an adult, and he's made a decision. You can't storm the castle and demand the wicked queen release the fair maiden."

Why did Henley have to make sense now of all times? He'd always been the impetuous one, encouraging Darwin to take chances.

"You're right," Darwin said through gritted teeth.

"You like him, don't you?" Henley asked tentatively.

"Well, yes, but—"

"I mean you *like* him."

Though he hated the amusement in Henley's tone, Darwin couldn't deny what he said was true. He *did* like Ricky. In their one interaction, he'd done more to relax Darwin than anyone had in a long time.

"I barely know him," Darwin replied, the words acrid on his tongue. He knew enough to admit Ricky made him laugh, set his stomach fluttering when he smiled. But admitting to feelings had Darwin stuck between two worlds. His love for Dean and his desire for the blond waiter.

"You hardly knew me when we kissed," Henley reminded him.

A quiet night, parents out for the evening, and the servants tucked in for the night. Two hormone-addled teens wondering what it would be like to have their first kiss. Darwin remembered the scene vividly. Even though he and Henley had known right away they were definitely not made for one another, it started them on the path to accepting who they were and, ultimately, had brought Darwin and Dean together for four years.

"It's not like that," Darwin protested, but the words didn't sound sincere, even to his own ears.

"But it could be, right? You want it to be?" Henley asked softly.

Darwin hated how perceptive Henley could be. As long as they'd known each other, it still surprised him when the wisecracking Henley turned serious. "I can fire you, you know," he grumbled.

"You can. You probably should. Hell, I'd fire me if I had the chance. Doesn't make it any less true. Since Dean died, you've thrown yourself into work. You start early in the morning and work until late at night. You don't make time for anything or anyone. One meal with Ricky and you're cancelling appointments to play mini-putts and eat food you've never tried before. I admit it's not the stuff of a life-long commitment, but it's a start."

The office door opened and Ricky stepped out, his mouth drawn into a grim line and his eyes red. Darwin glowered as Louisa called another server over, then pointed to the area in the rear of the restaurant. The waiter led Ricky to the back where they disappeared behind a dark wooden door.

"She fired him," he whispered to Henley.

"Then what will you do?" Henley prompted. "Are you going to let her fire him and watch as he walks away, or are you going to stand up for him?"

Anger surged through Darwin at Henley's questions. If a chance existed that there could be something between him and Ricky, he wanted to explore it. To do that, he couldn't let the man just leave, and he wouldn't let Louisa destroy his confidence over something that had been Darwin's fault. "I'm not going to be long, but why don't you go ahead and go. I'll wait for Ricky and take him home."

"Are you sure he won't go out through another door? Maybe an employee entrance?"

Darwin hadn't considered that. "Hang on," he told Henley, pulling the phone away from his ear. "Excuse me," he said to the hostess.

"Yes, Mr. Kincade?"

"Is there another door that employees exit from?"

"Yes, sir. We have a separate entrance for workers here."

"I'd like to speak to Ricky before he leaves."

The hostess glanced toward Louisa's office. "He has to come back up here," she told him. "Louisa will collect his ID badge, keys, and any property belonging to the restaurant."

"Thank you," he said. He stepped away from the desk, and returned to his call. "I'll be waiting for him," he told his friend.

"I can drive you both," Henley said.

What would Ricky say if he saw the limo and Henley? Darwin really didn't want to find out. He liked being just Darwin for a change, not the president of Kincade International, not one of the hundred wealthiest men in America under thirty-five. Just Darwin.

"It's fine. Go on home. If something comes up, I'll call you."

"Okay, if you're sure."

"I am. I'll see you in the morning."

He hung up and strode toward Louisa's office. He didn't bother to knock, choosing instead to make an entrance she wasn't likely to forget.

"What did you do?" he demanded.

She glanced up from the papers she had been going through, pushed out of the chair, and moved toward him. "Mr. Kincade, I'm sorry about what happened. We'll pay to have the suit cleaned, of course."

She reached out and put her hand on his arm, and Darwin glared at it. She thought the gesture gave her the upper hand. Not this time, though. Not by a long shot.

CHAPTER THREE

Ricky pulled his clothes from the locker and began stripping off his uniform. With each piece he took off, he imagined a weight being lifted. While he'd enjoyed the money he'd made, he had to admit the job wasn't really something he could see himself doing for a career. He had dreams, and he would bust his ass to see them realized.

"I'm sorry about this, Rick," Carter murmured.

Ricky turned to his…former coworker and grinned. "It's fine. She's been aching to fire me since not long after I started."

"At least you landed on your feet," Carter replied, a wide grin showing off his perfectly white teeth.

"What do you mean?" Ricky asked, sliding into his jeans.

"Mr. Kincade. He seems to like you."

"He's a nice guy."

"Hell yeah," Carter said, waggling his brows. "He's got a lot of nice things about him."

Before Ricky could ask what he meant, the door flew open and Sandra, the hostess, called out, "Carter, hurry. Mr. Kincade is in the office with Louisa, and we can hear them shouting from the dining room."

Ricky grabbed his uniform and his sneakers before he rushed from the locker room, Carter hot on his heels. He didn't want Darwin to get himself in trouble. It wasn't worth it. Not for him, and certainly not to go up against Louisa. He heard the patrons muttering about the shouting and quickened his pace. He'd almost reached the door when he heard Darwin's voice, breaking with anger.

"I don't give a *damn*," he shouted.

"Be reasonable," Louisa pleaded. "He wasn't working out."

He joined Carter and Sandra at the door, each of them straining not to miss a word Darwin and Louisa were saying. He leaned forward, then noticed he'd never finished dressing. He stepped behind his now former coworkers, and changed his shoes, while still listening to the conversation going on.

"Because you rode him. Nothing he did was good enough. You wanted to make him like Roy. Well, guess what? He's *not* Roy. In fact, he's a damn sight better than Roy ever was. He's pleasant and charming. He's got personality, which this place is sorely lacking."

It got quiet in the office for a few moments, and Ricky feared Darwin had pushed Louisa too far.

"This isn't about Roy. It's not even about Ricky. I run this restaurant. You better than anyone should know what that means," she yelled. "I don't own it. I'm responsible to the Berkhardts, so if you've got a better solution, please enlighten me. You can ask any of the staff. I expect perfection from each of them, because if they fail, I fail. And if that happens, I'm out the door, just as they would be."

"It was an *accident*," Darwin stressed.

"You think I don't know that?" Louisa shouted again. "He's a good kid. I like him a lot. But this isn't the place for someone like him. His third night on the job, he served Gregory Berkhardt and a friend of his from college. He always asks for the newest person, because he claims they're his barometer for how we're doing."

Ricky thought back and remembered the two men. They'd been drinking heavily and got upset when he suggested they might want to slow down and have an appetizer. The tall, dark man with the deep bloodshot eyes gave him a cold glare and asked if Ricky knew who he was. He hadn't, which increased the man's agitation even more.

"He told me to fire Ricky that night. He'd done nothing wrong, but no one refuses the Berkhardts. He and his friend had come in drunk, and when the bartender had cut them off for more alcohol, he told me to get them a table in the new guy's—Ricky's—station. I don't know if they thought they could bully him into getting them something, but he did exactly what he was supposed to do. I couldn't fire him for following the rules. Mr. Berkhardt told me I had to get it done." Ricky heard her sigh, which tore at his heart. He wished she had talked to him, because he would have quit before she risked her job for him.

Ricky swallowed hard. He glanced at Carter and Sandra, who still stood beside him as they listened intently at the door.

"I couldn't fire him," Louisa said again, her voice much softer this time. "I suggested this might not be the place for him, but he seemed very adamant that he could do this job. And he's good. The customers who've had him adore him. If I had to fire him, they'd have been upset. We might have lost their business, which would have pissed off Berkhardt even more.

"I...I wanted Ricky to quit. I didn't have the heart to take the job away from him, and if I told the people who requested him that he left, then the restaurant saved face. I thought, if he quit, he could think of me as a bitch, but he'd go with his head held high. But tonight I had to do what I'd been told. I hate it. He should have just left when he had the chance."

Carter whispered to Sandra, asking what they should do, but Ricky ignored them. He hadn't known any of the things Louisa had said, and regret caused his stomach to churn. He'd thought she hated him. Before Darwin could say anything, Ricky knocked at the door then pushed it open, Carter and Sandra scampering back to their stations. Darwin's face was an unhealthy shade of red, while Louisa's skin, which usually had a healthy glow, had turned pale.

"I have my locker cleaned out," Ricky said. "I know you have to fill out a lot of paperwork if you fire me, but what if I quit?"

Deep brown eyes peered at him. "You were listening," Louisa said, but she sounded sad instead of angry.

"Well, you were kind of loud," Ricky replied, trying to smile.

"I'm sorry," she said, the sincerity in her expression very telling. "I wish we could have made it work. I tried, I swear. But Berkhardt wanted you gone, and even though I protested the decision, he overruled me. I asked for time. I wanted to train you and show him that you were good at your job. It didn't matter. He didn't listen. So I'd hoped he'd been too drunk to remember his dictate. It didn't happen that way."

Darwin put a hand on Ricky's shoulder. "I'm sorry. I know you didn't want me to interfere, but I couldn't let it sit like this."

Ricky shrugged. "At least I know it had nothing to do with my skills."

"No, not at all," Louisa interjected. "Mr. Kincade was right. You were a breath of fresh air here. People complimented your attitude, your willingness to do what it took to make them happy. The night the Malchuck family came in, you calmed their little girl down when she got upset because she couldn't have chicken fingers. You made her a crown and declared her princess of the table. Mr. and Mrs. Malchuck wrote a letter that I put in your file, gushing about how you were an absolute doll, and how their daughter wants to come back so she can see you. When you go looking for a new job, please tell them to call me. I'll give you the best possible recommendation I can."

Warmth flooded Ricky. That made everything perfect for him. He'd be going out on a high note, because he'd made someone happy, which meant the world to him. He stepped away from Darwin, walked around the desk and wrapped his arms around Louisa's waist. She grabbed his shoulders and hugged him hard.

"I'm sorry," she murmured in his ear.

"I'm not," he told her. He stepped back, kissed her on the cheek, and placed his uniform on her desk. "Louisa, I'm here to quit."

She tried to smile, but couldn't quite do it. "I accept your resignation," she whispered, her eyes shining. "It was an honor to work with you."

"You, too," Ricky replied.

Darwin put a hand on Ricky's lower back and took him out of the restaurant through the front door. Ricky waved to a few people, who tried to smile at him, but he could tell their hearts weren't in it.

"I'm sorry," Darwin said again.

The pit that had formed in Ricky's stomach had vanished with the new information. Even though losing the job sucked, at least it hadn't been because he'd done something wrong.

"I'm okay," Ricky told him honestly. When they got to the sidewalk, Ricky turned to Darwin and asked, "So since I seem to have the night free, what do you think about going to get a drink?"

Ricky couldn't be sure if he'd agree. A look of puzzlement came over Darwin's face as if he had to think hard about the invitation. They stood for a few uncomfortable moments, before Ricky got the hint that Darwin didn't want to go.

"Hey, it's okay if you don't. I just thought I'd ask." Ricky tried to hide his disappointment. The thought of being alone after the stressful evening depressed him. When Darwin put a hand on his arm, Ricky turned and was graced with a beautiful smile.

"Sure, I think I'd like that," Darwin answered.

****

Darwin had met Dean at a business conference on his twenty-first birthday. The two of them had hit it off quickly when they'd found they had so much in common. Neither had been surprised when they fell into an easy friendship. Falling in love, though? That had been totally unexpected, but definitely not unwelcome. By his twenty-second birthday, Dean had moved into the mansion, and he and Darwin had begun a life together. Four years, and that hadn't been enough time at all.

When Ricky had asked Darwin out for a drink, he'd had no idea what to do. He'd never been one for social gatherings, and the thought that he could make a fool of himself and alienate Ricky terrified him. But when he'd seen Ricky's sad expression, he'd decided to take the chance.

Even though going out with Ricky wasn't a date, it still gave Darwin butterflies. From their initial meeting, he'd liked the man—self-assured, confident, and not unwilling to take Darwin to task, which he'd proven more than once. Darwin tried to relax as Ricky directed him to a bar not far from Asiago. As they strolled along the street, Ricky pointed out some of the shops.

"I like to see the new displays," he said. "I'd never be able to buy anything from places like these, but it's fun to look."

The bar was tucked between two of the shops Ricky said he loved. From the outside, the bright neon lights drew Darwin's attention. When they walked in, the first thing Darwin noted was that the couples on the dance floor were predominantly male. Darwin had never been to a gay bar, so if nothing else, being out with Ricky had certainly broadened his cultural horizons.

They took an empty booth near the center of the room.

"I want you to get the whole experience," Ricky told him, with a wave of his hand.

After he made sure Darwin was comfortable, Ricky asked him what he wanted to drink. He had been tempted to say Macallan M, but that seemed really out of place in this establishment. However, nothing else came to mind. He and Dean had never been drinkers, preferring to stay at home and keep each other company. Going out like this seemed terrifying, but exciting.

"What are you having?"

"There's a local cider I like," Ricky answered. "It's called Tempest Red Cider, and it's really good. They serve it in a chilled mug, so it's all frosty and cold."

"Okay, I'll give it a try."

He watched as Ricky strolled to the bar. In his street clothes, Ricky still possessed a certain grace when he walked. It seemed almost hypnotic the way Darwin couldn't take his eyes off the man. When Ricky brought the drinks to the table and put one in front of Darwin, he stared at the deep red liquid, with the tiny bubbles at the top. It reminded Darwin of a witch's brew. His expression must have given him away, because Ricky laughed and picked up his drink, then took a sip, before he smacked his lips theatrically.

"See? Not poisoned. Try it. If you don't like it, I'll get you something else."

Picking up the mug and bringing it to his lips, Darwin could smell the sweet concoction. His first taste, though, sold him completely. It tasted of apples, but had a definite kick to it.

"Good, huh?"

"Very. I'll have to see about picking some of this up."

"Don't bother," Ricky told him. "The bottled stuff isn't nearly as good. I'm not sure what the difference is, but it's really noticeable."

"Then perhaps I'll have to come back here again," Darwin said, hopeful that maybe Ricky'd come with him. He looked around; it seemed like a nice place. The bar itself appeared to be oak with brass trim. The decor suggested they'd had a hard time deciding on a theme and had gone for the hodgepodge approach, with a multitude of pictures and other items dotting the walls, none of which went well together. But it worked, at least to Darwin's mind.

There weren't many people in the bar, but it didn't matter. Darwin could sit with Ricky all night and simply listen as he told stories about people he'd served, some of the more risqué things that had happened with patrons in the restrooms, or the things that went on in the kitchen with the irascible chef. Enjoying someone else's company gave Darwin a warmth throughout his whole body.

As the night wore on, the place began to fill with more and more men, dressed in a variety of outfits—businessmen, guys in leather, college students with their school names emblazoned on their chests—and Ricky, with his open, friendly manner seemed to be able to be part of the whole lot.

Darwin had finished his first drink and had begun his second. Ricky's fourth had him slurring his words slightly, but beyond that, he seemed happy, which made everything okay. Darwin would make sure he made it home safely, even if he had to call Henley.

Ricky hiccupped, then grinned. He stared at Darwin for a few moments before he finally asked, "Do you maybe wanna dance with me?" He bit the corner of his lip, the uncertainty evident. Darwin could only describe the look as adorable. Ricky seemed to have so many facets, and Darwin hoped for time to explore them all.

Ricky's chuckle snapped Darwin from his reverie.

"So…dance?"

Dance? Darwin turned his attention to the lighted stage where a few men shimmied together, pressed against each other in erotic ways. He and his brother had been taught to waltz and other ballroom dances. While repetition had deeply engrained those lessons, he had no clue how to do what he saw on the stage.

"I…don't know how."

"No problem," Ricky said, grabbing Darwin's hand and leading him up to the raised dance floor. When they got there, Ricky leaned over and whispered in Darwin's ear, "Just let yourself go. You don't need to be great, or even good. Flow with the music."

The music, much louder on the dancefloor than it had been at the table, wrapped around them, the pulsating beat reverberating through his core. He lifted his arms and started to sway, shifting his hips side to side. He peeked over at Ricky who flowed like he had been made of liquid. Other men pushed in against them, and a knot started forming in Darwin's stomach. Why did it bother him so much to see men touching Ricky? Hell, Ricky didn't seem to mind their hands on him. Darwin tamped down the uncomfortable feelings and let the music take him away.

The volume dropped, and the bartender called out, "Closing time."

"Looks like we missed last call," Ricky said, his voice soft as he gazed at Darwin through his thick lashes.

Darwin wanted to protest. They hadn't even been there… Oh hell. The clock on the wall claimed it to be nearly two am. He'd been having such a good time he never even realized how quickly the evening had all passed.

"Well, that was….different." Darwin smacked himself internally. Different? Why not say the truth? It had been amazing. Sublime, even.

"I had a good time," Ricky said, guiding Darwin toward the door. He paused to say good night to the bartenders, who gave him hearty handshakes. "I love this place. They're some really great guys. Thanks for coming with me. I need to get home, though. Have to start looking for a new job tomorrow."

The door opened, and they stepped outside. Darwin glanced sideways toward Ricky. His shoulders had slumped a little, but whether from tiredness or the reminder he was no longer employed, Darwin didn't know.

I can get you a job. Whatever you want to do, I can help. The words were on the tip of Darwin's tongue, but he kept quiet. Ricky might appreciate the sentiment, but Darwin didn't think he'd actually take him up on it. He seemed too independent to take a handout. Truth be told, Darwin feared that if he offered Ricky a position, things between them would change, and Darwin didn't want that.

"Let me get you a cab," Darwin said, directing him to the taxi stand.

"Nah, it's a nice night. I think I'll walk. I only live a few blocks away. It's what made working at Asiago so cool."

Darwin didn't want the night to end. He couldn't remember having had so much fun in years. When Ricky bit his lip again, Darwin knew he had something on his mind. He took a step closer, ready to ask, when Ricky looked up, wrapped a gentle hand around Darwin's neck, and leaned forward to press their lips together. The kiss sent tingles down Darwin's spine. It had been so long since he'd last been kissed. He wrapped his arms around Ricky's waist, drawing him closer. When Ricky's tongue touched his lips, Darwin opened for him. He could taste the cider they'd consumed, but now it had a sweet and spicy taste to it that Darwin would gladly have every day.

When Ricky stepped back, Darwin didn't want to let him go. He wanted more with Ricky. More dancing. More drinking. More kissing.

"Can I call you?" Darwin asked, desperate for the night to not end.

"I'd be disappointed if you didn't," Ricky said, giving Darwin a sly grin.

They exchanged phone numbers, then Ricky gave Darwin one last peck on the lips and turned to walk away. Darwin shivered a little. He could happily watch Ricky walk until he disappeared from view but knew how awkward it would look if Ricky caught him. He stepped into the cab waiting at the taxi stand and told the driver where to take him. He smiled as he thought how Ricky had kissed him, and it had been damn nice. He hadn't been kissed by anyone since Dean, and he hadn't realized how much he'd missed it. He traced his lips with a fingertip and smiled. He hoped that there'd be more kisses in his future.

****

Ricky couldn't help but turn to watch as Darwin got into the cab. He really wanted to invite him up to his apartment, but Ricky had never been casual about sex. He liked a man who made him laugh, who acted protective of him, but still had an air of vulnerability. Darwin had those things in spades.

Ricky thought about texting Darwin before he got home, but decided he'd give the man a little space. They'd only known each other a short time, and Ricky didn't want to come off as needy or one of those people who had to know everything about someone. Besides, there had to be a little mystery in a relationship. What good would it do if everything spilled into the light within the first few days?

As he entered the lobby of his building, the smell of cabbage cooking caught his attention. He figured Mrs. Metzger must be getting ready for a visit from her son, and would be cooking for days before he arrived. He opened the mailbox and pulled out the small stack of envelopes. Deciding to forgo the elevator, he took the stairs two at a time, until he came to his floor.

"Merlin, I'm home," Ricky called as he entered his apartment and threw his keys and mail on the living room table. The tiny white fluff ball he'd found shivering on the sidewalk near his building stuck his head out from under the couch before bounding toward Ricky and trying to climb up his pant leg.

"Hey, you're frisky today," Ricky said, scooping the kitten into his hands and bringing their faces together. Merlin reached out and batted at Ricky's nose, which made him laugh. "Bet you're hungry, huh?" He started toward the kitchen. "Sorry I'm so late. Quit my job today, and then went out for a few drinks with Darwin. You'd like him. He's—"

Merlin mewed loudly.

"Okay, so not interested in my life. You only love me for the food, am I right?"

After putting Merlin down, Ricky opened the cabinet and pulled out a can of food with a dancing tuna on the front of it. He opened it and scooped it into a bowl, then set it on the floor. Merlin dove into it, eating voraciously.

"Slow down. You're going to get sick, and I'm the one who has to clean it up," Ricky admonished. Of course, Merlin ignored him completely. Ricky chuckled and went to sit down in the overstuffed chair he'd gotten at the thrift store. A little threadbare in places, but it still was his favorite. The fabric, with its muted blue and white checks, reminded him of the one his mom used to have when he was a kid. He pulled his legs up under him and grabbed the mail. Bills. Bills. Coupons. More bills. He sighed and tossed the stack back onto the table.

When the kitten finished his food, he loped over to Ricky, leapt up onto his leg, then climbed onto his chest, where he curled into a ball and made himself comfortable. Ricky stroked the kitten, delighting in the loud purr that emanated from the mound of fluff.

"Can I tell you about Darwin now?" Ricky whispered, rubbing the kitten between the ears. Merlin glanced up and yawned. "I'm going to take that as a yes, because I need to tell someone, and it's too late to call Trish."

His sister would be over the moon when he told her he'd met someone he liked. She'd always pushed him to get out and meet people, reminding him he'd never find a boyfriend if he holed up in his apartment alone. When he protested he wasn't alone, she told him Merlin didn't count.

"She was wrong," he said. "You're very important to me."

Merlin looked up and bumped his head against Ricky's chin, a gesture that always made Ricky smile.

"So, his name is Darwin. An interesting name, right? Don't find many of those around. He's between thirty and thirty-five, with dark hair, brown eyes, and a cute pug nose. His ears jut out just a little, but that adds to his personality, I think. He's different from the rest of the guys I've met. He's...sweet."

When Merlin started kneading Ricky's chest with those tiny claws of doom, Ricky decided the cat was implying they should get some sleep, though more likely he wanted additional food. Either way, Ricky was wrung out. He put the kitten on the floor and made his way to the bedroom. He stripped off his shirt, which he tossed into the hamper as he passed by the bathroom. After removing his shoes, socks, and pants, he crawled into the bed, allowing the soft, lumpy mattress to envelop him. He waited a few moments, then felt the tug on the blanket as Merlin made his way onto the bed and settled on Ricky's pillow.

"Good night, boy," Ricky said quietly, before he drifted off into a dreamless sleep.

CHAPTER FOUR

Darwin glanced at his watch and suppressed a groan. He told Heather to schedule his brother, but eight a.m. on a Monday? Maybe this had been revenge for making her reschedule. Or maybe Kent hadn't been able to come the previous week. At least they'd agreed to meet at Kincade, so Darwin didn't have to travel. Though when he'd walked into the building and found Kent's group waiting and looking none too happy about it, he'd known it would be a very long day.

Kent had been droning on for an hour, talking about how his company's product would revolutionize not only individual houses around the world, but whole cities. Darwin loved his brother, but the man had made and lost several fortunes, starting with his inheritance, whenever something shiny attracted his attention. He'd throw money, hand over fist, at any new adventure. On occasion, his enthusiasm worked out, and Kent reaped enormous profits, but more often than not, his brother could have tossed his money into a pit then covered it with manure and been better off.

At thirty-six, Kent was the older brother by three years, but he certainly didn't look it. With his dark hair and deep brown eyes, people often mistook them for twins instead of simply siblings. Growing up, his brother had always been a doer, always chasing the next big thing. He'd excelled in school, and they'd both thought he'd inherit the family business when their parents died. Darwin had no idea which of them was more surprised when their parents had named Darwin CEO instead of Kent at their father's retirement party.

"So what you're telling me is that I have to bail you out," Darwin finally said as Kent wound down his presentation.

The members of the KK Enterprises board turned to one another and began to whisper, occasionally glancing between Kent and Darwin. A few of them straightened their paperwork nervously. Darwin's stomach knotted at the thought of being in this position. He dreaded telling Kent no, because he felt certain their relationship wouldn't survive. So far though, nothing in Kent's presentation had swayed Darwin's opinion. The fact that his own board had told him they'd back whatever decision he made hadn't helped in the least. But as always, the buck stopped with him, and he wouldn't risk Kincade International or the wellbeing of his employees on guilt of potentially widening the rift that existed between Darwin and his sibling.

"Well, no, not bail us out," Kent replied, scratching his head. "More like invest in our company. It will help keep everyone employed while we work to develop this product."

As he scrubbed a hand across his face, Darwin tried to figure out what he would tell his brother. The product he pushed seemed like crap—putting it nicely. While making their products more environmentally friendly had been something he stressed at Kincade, Kent's idea involved a composting garbage disposal. On the surface, it did seem like a viable product, but further study showed that unlike other companies that had invested considerable time and effort into making and marketing their product, the people Kent had gotten involved with had cut too many corners, making the product cheap and unreliable.

"How much did you spend on this?" Darwin asked.

"That's the great thing. I got in for only one point three million dollars. This thing will be worth a hundred times that."

Darwin groaned and slumped in his chair. He couldn't believe Kent's board would actually go along with this idea. He took a moment to look around the table, the expectant faces staring at him. Eight men and two women surrounded the large oval table, with Darwin at one end and the rest of them huddled on the other side.

The fact that his brother stood in front of him, and with the backing of his board, pitched an idea that would never work viably made Darwin wonder how much trouble they were actually in.

"I'm sorry, Kent. I'm afraid we're going to have to say no."

Kent's expression spoke volumes—hurt, anger, and pain.

"Can you excuse us, people?" Kent asked his board members. They stood, gathered their papers, and shuffled out of the room. Darwin could hear their murmured words as they passed by—he was arrogant, cared for no one but himself, how could he turn his brother away—but their condemnation didn't change the facts. The decision hadn't been personal. He'd always given Kent anything he'd asked for.

Kent should have been running the family corporation. He studied hard, got good grades, but then it all went downhill fast after he fell in with some friends who were only interested in having a good time. That started the problems between their family, which finally culminated in Darwin being named CEO. When he'd taken the reins, Darwin had known next to nothing. He'd depended heavily on his staff to teach him day-to-day operations. Kent wouldn't have needed to do that. But his brother hadn't been given the company, Darwin had.

"So you're just going to say no, huh?" Kent demanded as he stormed across the room, coming to a stop at the large picture window that gave a magnificent view of Lake Michigan. "You aren't even going to look at the proposal?"

Darwin sighed. "I did. I went through everything you sent me with a fine-toothed comb. On paper, the concept sounds amazing, but the company's track record speaks for itself. They're not developing the product as they claimed. They're looking for a sucker to take it off their hands, and you walked in and gave them exactly what they needed."

"Because I can make something of it," Kent promised. "Their idea is sound, but I know they gave up on it too early. I want to take this and make something out of it. My R & D team tells me that with a few changes, they can turn it into something that will have a huge impact on companies and communities that are struggling to be more green. To do that, we—I—need your help." Kent paused for a minute, resting his head against the glass. He took a deep breath, turned around, and said, "Take over my company, become chairman, whatever, but we need this project to keep our people employed. I'll step down or do something else, but don't hurt them. They've worked so hard on this, and they're so close to perfecting it."

Over the years, Kent had given many impassioned speeches, but the words were always about how it would impact him—how he could do something and make it better. This Kent? Darwin couldn't be sure he'd ever met this man. He'd known his brother long enough to be sure of his sincerity, and that made his next words easy to say.

Darwin sucked in a deep breath, stood, and leveled his gaze at Kent. "I'll give you one year. We'll give KK Enterprises an injection of funds once, and, Kent, be sure you understand this will be the only time. I'm not going to ask you to give up on this fool's errand, but if you're serious about keeping your company afloat, this isn't the way to do it."

Kent rushed toward Darwin and hugged him tightly for a moment, then he stepped back, his excitement plain to see. "You don't know what this means. We can make this work. I know we can. I have an incredible team behind me, and they all say the same thing: Gen-tech has a great product, but they mothballed it and never looked beyond their own ideas for it. Our plans are to take it in a different direction. Make it something viable and, hopefully, moneymaking."

His brother's expression told Darwin he had another idea for the disposal beyond what his plans called for. He had a moment of panic as he thought about how Kent might have played him, but he didn't think so. He had never seen Kent this excited about a project. In fact, this Kent seemed…different. More sure of himself, but still more comfortable in his skin than Darwin remembered. Maybe he would be throwing good money after bad, but he wanted to trust Kent.

"I'll get Heather to have legal draw up the contracts," Darwin said, the words heavy from his mouth. "Remember, this is a one-time investment. I don't know how you're going to pull off this miracle, but I hope to hell it works out for you."

"It will," Kent promised. "When we announce it to the press, I want you there with me. Without you, none of this would be possible. Thank you isn't strong enough to show our appreciation." Then he paused, dropped his head, and placed his hands on the conference table. Darwin took a seat next to him and watched as Kent slid his fingers across the polished surface. "Dee, do you want to take over the company? I know I said you could, and if you want it, then it's yours."

His brother used to call him Dee when they were kids, but he hadn't done it in years. Kent continued to surprise him. Before Kent had started KK Enterprises, the two of them had fallen out over their parents naming Darwin successor of the company, and other than giving him what amounted to a severance package, they'd basically left Kent out in the cold. Darwin had tried to talk to him on numerous occasions, to explain he'd known nothing about their plan and would be glad to name them co-owners, but his brother's stubborn attitude had made conversation impossible.

Then came the day Kent had announced he'd started a new company. Darwin's pride had been overshadowed by the fact Kent had showed up at his door looking for skilled personnel. He'd demanded Darwin allow him to speak to the employees, so they could decide which Kincade they wanted to work for. Kent had argued he should be allowed the opportunity since their parents had forced him to start over on his own.

Darwin had fumed at the outrageous request. He'd told Kent in no uncertain terms that he didn't have a legal leg to stand on, and that he would not allow him to speak with the employees. Kent's anger had been a sight to behold. Before Darwin could call security to have him removed, Kent had stormed off, vowing to never speak to Darwin again. The thought he'd lost his brother caused Darwin's

OF LOVE AND CORN DOGS

heart to ache, but he knew he'd done nothing to warrant Kent's anger.

Six months later, Kent had been arrested for drunk driving, and he'd called Darwin to bail him out. He'd talked about the situation with Dean, who'd told him that he should see the call as Kent's olive branch, an opportunity to start mending their fences. Grudgingly, Darwin had gone.

That had started the new phase of their relationship. Kent had told him he no longer wanted to be a part of Kincade International. He'd insisted he understood why their parents had named Darwin as their successor instead of him, and that he wanted to become his own man, free of the shadow of their shared name. While Darwin had wanted to protest that Kent's name had opened the door for him to start his own company, he'd bit his tongue and stayed silent.

Their relationship had thawed after that, though it had never returned to what they'd had as kids when Kent had accepted with dignity, if not outright acceptance, his younger brother tagging along everywhere. But, at least now they talked on occasion.

For Kent to stand there today and offer his company to Darwin proved one thing: the man before him was *not* the same guy who had been so distant for so many years.

"No, I don't want to take over your company. It's your life's work, and I love seeing you passionate about this, especially the part where you're going to take care of your people first."

Kent ducked his head slightly, then slid into one of the chairs at the meeting table. "I understand now, you know," he said softly. "For you, it's always been about the people. For me, it's been the profit at any cost. Making myself look good, even though others were doing the work. It's why Mom and Dad left the family business to you, because you shared their vision. I didn't. I've been a real asshole to you, and I hope you'll be able to forgive me one day."

Darwin surreptitiously pinched his leg to prove he wasn't dreaming. The pain cleared his head a little. "You're serious?"

"As a heart attack. Mila took me to task one day after we unveiled some product. I don't even remember what it was. She told me how ashamed she was when I stood in front of everyone and told them about *my* new product. She said every word out of my mouth was either my, me, or, at one point, Kent Kincade. There's nothing quite like talking about yourself in the third person to piss off your wife." Kent shook his head and chuckled.

Darwin loved Mila—long dark hair, lashes most women would kill for, and a figure that had many men assuming she was merely a trophy wife. She set them straight with a business acumen that showed people she shouldn't be underestimated. She'd earned the position of COO.

"She told me flat out that if I couldn't see the people who had worked so hard to make the item, the ones who helped to get it ready, or hell, even the janitors who cleaned up after every shift, then she didn't want to be a part of the company. She walked out of our house that night, angrier than I'd ever seen her. I wasn't sure if she'd left me, the company, or both.

"I sat there, seeing the constant reminders of her, and realized how lost I would be if I never got her back. Then as I went up to the bedroom, I passed by her office. She had her laptop open, something she never does. My guess is that she'd done it intentionally, but she denies it. Anyway, I went in to look. Did you know she had a file on *every* employee? Birthdates, spouse names, anniversaries, kid's names and ages, hobbies. A huge list of facts about everyone who worked for KK Enterprises and their family. If you introduced me to Megan Jones, who'd been with the company for three years, I would have had no clue who the hell she was. Mila did. She made it her business to know. So I sat down at the workstation and started going through what she had."

Darwin watched as his brother spoke about the things he'd learned. His expression shifting from discomfort to acceptance of his journey of discovery. This lesson had been sorely needed. He wished that Kent could have learned it from their parents, but the fact that

Mila finally got through to him showed him that maybe his brother really had turned his business and his life around. He sure wished it could be so. He had a glimmer of hope that maybe this new Kent could be counted as a brother again, instead of a distant acquaintance.

Kent began counting off on his fingers, his expression pained. "Tom Kennedy came to work for us because his son had leukemia and he needed good insurance. Martin Torrance lost his wife about a year after he started working for us. Ann Jameson's son graduated at the top of his class in high school and would be off to MIT the following year. Her calendar had notes of who to call, who to send cards to, and stuff I don't even understand. I knew her secretary helped keep it all up to date and organized, and I wanted to thank her, but then I realized...I didn't even know the woman's name. Hell, I was shocked when I found out it was a man named Tony, and I'd talked to him several times.

"I called Mila that night and told her how sorry I was. How much of a bastard I'd been, how callous, how she should have better. And it dawned on me. This was what made Mom and Dad so successful. They cared about their employees, and they showed it. I didn't. Martin's wife got a huge bouquet of flowers for her funeral because Mila sent them. Ann Jameson's son got a congratulations card with a five-hundred-dollar gift certificate. If the only reason Tom Kennedy stayed with us was for insurance, then something had to change. *I* had to change. And I promised Mila I would."

And Kent had. Now that he looked beneath the exterior, Darwin could see the change. His brother wore it well. Where before he'd been driven to prove how great Kent could be, now he cared about his employees. He seemed to be learning how important a good crew was to the success of a company. Without his own people, Darwin never could have made it past the first year. When his parents had died, he couldn't have been more adrift. But his staff knew their jobs, they were patient with him, willing to help him learn every aspect of their responsibilities, so that he knew what they did.

"Mila came home that night, and over the next few months, she and I spent hours together so I could learn who worked for me. Do you know that Robert Carson cried when I wished him a happy birthday? He worked for us for six years. He'd been responsible for eight of the products we had on the market, and I didn't even know the man's name. I invited him to lunch, and we talked about what he'd been working on. His excitement excited *me*.

And Darwin could see it in every gesture Kent made, hear it in each word, and his heart beat a little faster at the changes he witnessed. *This* Kent would have been given Kincade, no doubt. Their parents would have been so damn proud to see how the two of them had grown up.

"I went home that night and kissed my wife like she should always be. I told her that she had to be the most amazing person on the planet to put up with someone who had an ego my size, and that I didn't deserve her at all. And I made an admission that should have landed me in divorce court. I told her that when I married her, it had been solely for her looks. It took me months to realize the brains that she had, too. And that realization had me offering her the COO job. Best decision ever."

"And what did she say when you told her you'd married her for her looks?"

Kent blushed. "She stroked a finger over my chin, then told me she'd married me for the same reason."

Darwin broke out with a laugh. "I'm really glad things are going your way. There is one thing that Mila worked out that Mom and Dad never did. Our parents made the employees feel valued, but never really gave them the chance to feel like family. When I started, I wanted to bring them in on more things, let them know their opinions mattered as much as their loyalty. I started holding monthly lunches, where we'd sit and talk. No business, just about how things were going. I think it made a huge difference."

Kent nodded. "Mila is teaching me about respecting the people who work for us. Turnover has dropped, employee morale is at an all-time high, and they're always exceeding their quotas." He ducked his head again. "I wish I had learned that years ago. Who knew Mom and Dad were on to something?"

Darwin checked his watch again. He'd been so comfortable talking to Kent he'd completely forgotten that the board of directors for KK Enterprises waited in the hallway. He stood, Kent following suit.

"Your people are outside," he reminded his brother.

Kent sighed. "Can't we just forget they're there? I'm finally talking to you like I should have years ago. I'm so sorry for all the shit I piled on you. You didn't do anything to earn it at all."

Darwin's heart swelled. He'd been angry at his brother's animosity, but he missed having Kent in his life. He threw himself at his brother and clung tight to his waist. It wasn't businesslike, but he didn't care. There'd been many times since Dean died that he'd wished he could talk to Kent. He'd even picked up the phone a time or two. He wasn't sure if it had been pride or stupidity that had made him put it back down. Probably both.

"I miss you, Darwin," Kent whispered, his breath blowing against Darwin's ear.

"Me, too."

The two men broke the clench and stepped back. Darwin wondered if Kent felt as awkward as Darwin did.

"Before we let them back in and tell them you'll give us a transfusion—and just so we're clear, I won't ask a second time, I promise—tell me something that I've missed because I had to go be stubborn."

Darwin thought for a moment. He knew what he wanted to say, but he wasn't sure if he was ready to share his news with anyone other than Henley at the moment. He peered at his brother and saw nothing but honest curiosity. Darwin drew in a deep breath.

"There's this restaurant I used to go to. It's called Asiago—"

"I took Mila there for our anniversary. They've got great seafood."

"Yeah, it also had a waiter named Roy."

He waited for his brother's reaction. When he said nothing, Darwin plowed ahead.

"Long story short. I went there each week to look at him. He was sexy, but a bit dry. Then a couple weeks ago, he was gone and I had a new waiter. He made me laugh. He…" Darwin stopped. He wasn't sure how to talk to Kent about this.

"Made you feel something you haven't in a long time?"

Darwin nodded.

Kent gripped Darwin's shoulder. "That's a good thing. I know you miss Dean, but he wouldn't have wanted you to lock yourself away. He would want you to get out and meet someone, and I think you know it."

Darwin did. He and Dean had talked about it when they'd found out he didn't have much time left. He'd insisted Darwin do his best to find a new love. But Darwin couldn't bring himself to do it. Every look in Roy's direction felt like a dishonor to Dean's memory. But then Ricky appeared and tore through every defense Darwin had built around his heart. He had no idea how. They'd only seen each other two times, but it had been enough that Darwin wanted to know more.

"So about Asiago?" Kent prompted, pulling Darwin from his thoughts.

"I met someone. His name is Ricky," Darwin said on a sigh.

CHAPTER FIVE

After he and Kent had let the board members back into the meeting room and told them there would be an infusion of cash, Kent had stayed to catch up a little more. They'd gone to Darwin's office and talked, Kent being every bit the big brother. Darwin wouldn't deny how good their new tentative bond felt.

"It's never easy, is it?" Kent asked, sitting on the plush black couch in the middle of Darwin's office. Darwin cracked a new bottle of Macallan M from the cabinet above the small wooden bar he kept for when clients came to talk business. He poured them each a shot to celebrate the saving of Kent's company, as well as the two of them working to iron out their problems.

"What's that?" Darwin asked.

"This," he replied, waving his hand around the large office suite. "You come in here every day, work your butt off, and then at night, Henley takes you home so you can start all over again. That can't be what you want out of life, is it?"

Darwin's throat closed up, so he simply shook his head.

"Being alone for so long isn't healthy. I know you've got people around you, but it isn't the same. They're family, and I'm starting to understand that, but do you feel comfortable talking to them about personal matters like this?"

"No," Darwin whispered, his voice harsh. He placed his rocks glass on the marble side table beside his seat. He glanced over at his brother, expecting to find pity. Instead, he saw understanding.

"I know we're just starting to mend the fences, but if you ever need to talk to someone, you can call me. If you don't want to talk to me, Mila would be more than happy to hear from you."

His eyes burned, and Darwin knew tears wouldn't be far behind. He hadn't cried for years over Dean's loss, and the memories had faded a bit with time, but now he could picture him, clear as anything. His smile, which always warmed Darwin's heart. His eyes, which twinkled with mischief. And his arms, which had given Darwin comfort, even when they'd known their time together would soon run out.

"I'm afraid," Darwin admitted.

Kent slid closer to where Darwin sat. He reached out and put a hand atop Darwin's. The warmth chased away the chill that the liquor couldn't touch.

"I get that. It's scary putting yourself out there again. What if he doesn't like you? What if it doesn't work out? But stop asking that. Think about what happens if it does. You've got to take the chance, because if you don't, you're only going to have a life filled with more regrets. And those are a worse hurt than if things go wrong, believe me."

Darwin straightened in his chair. He stopped thinking about himself for a minute and gazed at his brother. He could see the sadness in his eyes, and Darwin recognized it for what it was. He'd seen that look many times when he'd stared at his own reflection. Kent now lived with the regret of their parents' final years. The attitude he'd developed, which caused a schism to form in the family.

"Mom and Dad loved you, you know."

Kent gave a half shrug. "I gave them enough reasons not to. In my mind, I had money, I had friends, and we could party from sunup to sundown. But that life got old after a while. The thrills didn't come as easily. People wanted more from me. To buy them things, take them places. Before I realized it, I had lost myself and didn't really care if I came back from it. I disappointed our parents and you. And it seemed easier to just let it go than try to fight to get it back."

He had never seen Kent in that light. To Darwin, he'd always been a scrapper, fighting for what he believed he'd been due. Saying he'd given up hurt Darwin's heart, because in all honesty, that was what he'd done after Dean died. Maybe he and his brother weren't so dissimilar after all.

"When Mom and Dad told me they were going to make me head of the company, I protested. I told them it should be you, not me. They each gave me a sad smile and told me that you were on a journey right now, and that until you decided it was finished, it might be some time before you came back."

"They were right. I wouldn't have if I hadn't met Mila. She gave me so much shit when we got together, because she knew I had potential. And even then I misused that."

"Meh. She got you whipped into shape," Darwin replied, grinning.

"She did at that. Which brings us back to the subject at hand. You like this guy, right?"

Darwin nodded. Logically, he knew it made no sense, but he truly did like Ricky. He had an air about him that had Darwin aching to know more. The kiss they shared had thrown open doors Darwin thought he'd closed off long ago. Heat surged to Darwin's cheeks as his thoughts took an erotic turn. He glanced at Kent, hoping his embarrassment wasn't obvious. Kent let go of Darwin's hand and stood.

"Then find out where it's going to go. Don't hold back. Even if it doesn't work out with Ricky, it might work out with the next man, or the next. There has to be more to your life than work." Kent gave Darwin a strange look, and then he laughed.

"What's so funny?"

"I just realized. You are all about work. I was all about finding ways to not work. Now I'm the one who is trying to take the job more seriously, while you're trying to find a way to finally think about yourself. We're a fine pair."

Darwin sat in the back of the limo later that afternoon, fiddling with his phone. Heather had blocked the whole day for the meeting with Kent, and as soon as his brother had left, Darwin told Heather he would take the remainder of the afternoon off. He reminded her he would be reachable by phone if she needed him. She'd seemed surprised, but then smiled at him. He hadn't left work early in years, but after the emotional roller coaster he'd been on lately, he decided he'd earned a break. The weather seemed lovely, and he hadn't gotten out much, so he asked Henley to drive him through the park to look at the beautiful flower displays.

As they drove he scrolled through the contacts until he got to Ricky's number. They hadn't spoken in a week, and Darwin wanted to use the excuse he'd been busy, but in truth, he feared Ricky would change his mind.

The window that separated the driver from the back of the car rolled down, startling Darwin. He hated when Henley had it up, because it made him feel isolated.

"Are you going to use the phone, or are you content playing with it?"

Darwin pulled a face. "Are you actually talking about the phone, or is this one of your famous euphemisms?"

Henley chuckled. "I can see it working either way, so use whichever you're most comfortable with."

"So what do you think? Kent says I should call Ricky, but I'm nervous."

An expression Darwin couldn't recall ever seeing before passed over Henley's face, but just as quickly, it vanished. "I think you should call him. Get to know the man. Find out if there is anything between the two of you. From what I saw, he's a nice guy, and you need a little nice in your life."

Darwin fiddled with the phone once more before he drew in a deep breath and pushed connect. After four rings, it went to voice mail.

"Hi, Ricky. It's me. Um, I mean, it's Darwin. I was calling to see how you were doing. Talk to you later."

He hung up and dropped his head back against the seat. He could see Henley grinning at him in the rearview mirror.

"Man, you are so out of practice," his friend teased.

"No kidding," Darwin agreed. He slipped the phone into his pocket and tried to pretend the wait wouldn't kill him.

***

Ricky walked out of another restaurant where he'd finished applying. He groaned as the heat once again washed over him. If one thing bugged Ricky, heat would be it, and the weather report had said it would be warmer than normal from today—Monday—through Friday. He sweated easily, and the fact he'd worn the only suit he owned didn't help. He'd done it just in case he got asked to stay for an interview. But that hadn't happened. Again.

He'd left applications at twelve restaurants in the last week and none of them had called him back. After he turned his phone back on, he pulled up his online bank statement and grimaced. He'd have enough money for this month, but once he paid the bills, his student loans, and rent, there wouldn't be much there for those pesky incidentals, like food. He had to find a job and soon.

He had just put his phone away when he heard the tone that indicated a voice message. He slipped it out of his pocket and saw he had missed a call from Darwin. His heart leapt just a little bit. He had waited to see if the man would call, but wasn't sure what proper protocol was after their not-quite-a-date. Call and invite Darwin out? Wait to see if Darwin called him? He groaned. It was like high school all over again. Maybe it would be easier to write a note with '*Do you like me?*' and checkboxes for yes or no.

He listened to the message, smiled, and put the phone away. He wiped the sweat from his brow, sighed as he looked up, hoping to see a few rainclouds that might bring some much needed relief from the heat. Of course, not a cloud in the sky. The sun beat down, heating everything to well past the ninety degrees his phone claimed it was. He started the long twelve-block walk to his apartment. After the first two blocks, he had to peel off the suit coat and long-sleeve shirt he'd worn in hopes of getting an interview. His T-shirt dripped with sweat and he thought about taking that off, too, but he figured he'd wait until he got home and strip off in the privacy of his room. At least then he could sit in front of the tiny air conditioner in the bedroom, where he would then pretend it wasn't really that hot.

Stepping into his place, he caught sight of Merlin sprawled out on Ricky's favorite chair, on his back, legs spread in the near sweltering heat. He scooped the kitten into his arms, then strode off to the bedroom where he closed the door, then cranked the small AC unit he'd found in a thrift store as high as he could. He put Merlin on the bed, then grinned as the cat jumped on the machine and stretched across the vent.

"Sorry, buddy. I know it's hot. It's supposed to cool off next week. I know that doesn't help now, though. When I go out tomorrow, I'll leave the air on so you can try to stay comfortable." Ricky groaned at the thought of his electric bill, but he refused to leave Merlin in an apartment that would probably be a few degrees warmer than outside.

Stripping off his clothes, Ricky trudged to the bathroom and turned on the shower. He stepped beneath the cool jets of water, grateful for even that little bit of relief. After toweling off, he joined Merlin in the bedroom, stretched out naked on the bed, and sighed. The little AC unit didn't put out much cool air, but almost anything was better than being outside. At least coming home had been a welcome relief.

He rolled to his side and reached into the pocket of his discarded pants to pull out his phone. He listened to Darwin's message again, chuckling at how nervous he sounded.

"What do you think, Mer? Should I call him back or make him sweat it out?"

The cat gave a soft meow.

"Yeah, that's what I thought, too."

He dialed the number, then gave a soft whimper when it went to voice mail.

"Hey, it's Ricky. I see we're playing phone tag, so I guess this means you're it. Talk to you later."

He hung up, put the phone on the nightstand, and closed his eyes, wishing he and Merlin could be in Alaska right now.

***

As the car pulled out of the tunnel, Darwin's phone beeped. He dropped it once before he could get a good grip on it. When he saw Ricky's name, heat rushed through him.

"Damn," Darwin cursed. "I missed his call!"

"Okay, so you call him back. It's not a big deal, Dare. Why are you so nervous about this?"

"It's been a few years," he snapped. "I'm out of practice."

"And right now, you're acting like a teenager instead of an adult. Suck it up, buttercup. Call him back."

Darwin wanted to protest, but he couldn't deny it. He *felt* like a teen—gawky, unsure, and more than a little nervous. He sucked in a quick breath to steady himself, then called Ricky back.

"'Lo?"

He could hear the hum of a machine in the background, and Ricky sounded like he'd been sleeping. "Hey, it's Darwin."

"Hey," Ricky replied, now seemingly more alert. "How you doing?"

"Did I wake you?"

"Nah, not really." Ricky yawned, and Darwin stifled a giggle at how cute the noise sounded. "Just dozing in the air conditioning. It's hotter than hell outside today."

Darwin leaned forward to peek at the digital readout on the dash and winced. Ninety-four degrees.

"Are you okay?"

"Yeah, just warm. So what's going on?"

"Not much. I figured I should call you to see what you were up to."

Ricky sighed. "Well, let's see. I haven't found a job yet. Applied at a bunch of places, but no one has called me back. Beyond that, I've been pretty much a homebody. I can't afford to go out, so I'm sitting at home and playing with Merlin."

"Merlin?"

"He's my kitten. I found him on my way home one night about three months ago. No clue where he came from. He just, *poof*, appeared on the sidewalk."

Darwin bit his tongue. He didn't want to make Ricky uncomfortable, but damn it, he didn't want him to be out on the street either.

"Is there anything I can do for you? I mean if you need money or something…"

He heard Ricky suck in a breath, before he gave his frosty answer. "No, we're fine."

"Sorry. I just… If you need help, I hope you'll let me know."

"Thanks," Ricky said quietly. "We're really okay, though. But it's nice that you asked."

"So, listen. I was wondering if you wanted to go out tonight. With me, I mean. We can go to dinner or something."

"Thanks, but I have to say no," Ricky replied, his voice tight. "I really don't have any money to spare right now."

"My treat. You bought me drinks at the club, so it's my turn to take you out."

"Yeah?"

Relief flooded Darwin. Ricky hadn't simply said no. "Absolutely."

Darwin could hear the smile in Ricky's voice when he replied, "Okay, sure. I'd like that."

"I'll pick you up at seven?" Darwin asked, tamping down hard on the urge to yell he'd gotten a date.

"Sounds good."

Ricky rattled off his address, which Darwin wrote on his notepad.

"See you tonight," he whispered, even though Ricky had already disconnected.

"Darwin's got a date," Henley teased. "Do we need to swing by the pharmacy to get you some protection? Wait. Do you even remember how to use it? We might have to pick up some bananas, so I can show you the proper way to put on a condom."

"You know how sometimes you say things and they're absolutely hilarious?" Darwin asked, meeting Henley's eyes in the rearview mirror. "This isn't one of them."

"Ouch. Cut down in my prime," Henley complained, clutching his heart dramatically with one hand. Then he laughed. "I assume you want to go home now, so you can get ready. Where are we picking him up?"

Panic surged through Darwin. He hadn't even considered that Henley would expect to drive them.

"Didn't you have plans for tonight?"

"Meh. I thought about binge watching something on Netflix, but if you want to go out, I'd rather do that."

Darwin gave a nervous chuckle. "You go ahead and kill some brain cells. We can take a taxi. I'm not sure how late we'll be out, and there's no sense in you waiting up for me."

Henley shrugged. "I don't mind. I don't get out much, so this gives me a chance to stretch my legs. While you guys eat, I can take a walk around the block or something."

He didn't want Henley coming along. He wanted it to be him and Ricky. He wanted to be together, just the two of them. Ricky had kissed him, so he must like him. But would that change if he found out Darwin wasn't the man he thought? What did his parents used to say? Money changes everything.

"No, it's okay. The cab is fine. Besides, Maria is making stuffed cabbage rolls tonight, and I know how you get if you miss them."

Henley's eyes went wide. "Really? Hell, yeah. You take a cab. Since you're going out, can I have yours, too?"

A laugh bubbled out of Darwin, equal parts relief and amusement.

"Want me to call her and have her make a double batch?"

"Since you're the only one she'll listen to, yes, please. And if she wants to make some buns to go with it, I'd be down for that."

Darwin threw out a prayer of thanks to the universe then turned his attention to the matter at hand. Where could he take Ricky that would be nice but not ostentatious?

When the cab pulled up to Ricky's apartment, Darwin sighed. The building seemed nice enough, even if it didn't offer central air. He could see Ricky living here. Like his date, it had an earthy charm to it. With cream-colored brick and large windows that would let in a lot of light, it looked inviting.

As he stepped into the lobby of the building, he took notice of the faded art deco elevator doors and gave a low whistle. At one time, this building must have been considered high class. As much as he would love to check the history of the place, he had come for one reason.

He pushed the button for Ricky's apartment. The speaker buzzed and Ricky said he would be down in a minute. Darwin shivered despite the heat. How long had it been since he'd been on a date? Damn. He couldn't remember where he and Dean had gone. The fact saddened him. His stomach clenched as memories of Dean came crashing down. Maybe he hadn't really been ready for this.

When the elevator door opened and Ricky stepped out, all other thoughts went out of Darwin's head. He had on dark jeans and a light green shirt that offset his eyes beautifully. His blond hair, a bit longer than Darwin had seen him with before, had been artfully styled by liberal use of sculpting gel. The sight took Darwin's breath away.

"H-hi," Darwin stuttered.

"Hey." He glanced at Darwin, then down at his own clothes. "Are you sure I'm dressed okay? I mean my clothes aren't nearly as nice as yours."

"You're gorgeous," Darwin replied, then snapped to attention. "I mean you look great. Seriously. For where we're going, I'm probably overdressed. I just couldn't make up my mind between the 'dress to impress' or 'dress down so he might think I'm cool' look. As you can see, I made the wrong choice."

Darwin's voice sounded husky, even to him. He wanted to send the cab away and order a pizza or something, because sitting in a public place with Ricky, trying to make interesting conversation while drooling like the village idiot had now become a real possibility.

"I think you look great," Ricky told him, a smile on his lips as his gaze raked over Darwin's form. "I've half a mind to ask if you want to forget about going out and stay here."

"We could do that," Darwin replied, trying not to appear overenthusiastic.

Ricky chuckled. "We could, if my apartment weren't so damn hot. I swear, it's ten degrees warmer in there than outside. Merlin has camped out on the AC unit, and I think if we try to get him to move, he might do us some serious harm. He may be small, but he's got some sharp claws."

Darwin grinned then gestured toward the door. "Point taken. We wouldn't want to displace the cat. If you're ready, our chariot awaits."

Ricky moved with a graceful sway of his hips. To call it enticing would be a gross understatement. Darwin rushed forward and opened the door for Ricky, then pulled open the cab door as well.

"You do know I can open doors, right?" Ricky asked, but the slight quirk of his lips clued Darwin in to the fact he didn't mind the gesture at all.

The first part of the cab ride had taken place in relative silence once Darwin told the driver where they were going. He held his hands on his knees to keep them from bouncing and kept his eyes glued to the window so Ricky wouldn't see how freaked out his date had gotten.

"You sure you want to do this?" Ricky whispered.

Darwin's gaze snapped to him. "Yes! Why? Don't you?" *Please say yes. Please say yes.*

"I do. But you seem so nervous. If you're uncomfortable, we can go another time."

Taking a deep breath, which he exhaled slowly, Darwin tried for a smile. "I'm sorry. It's been a while since I've been out, and I'm really, *really* out of practice. I don't want to do or say anything that will have you regretting the choice to come with me."

Ricky put his hand atop Darwin's. "I don't regret it at all. I promise." He leaned forward and gave Darwin a peck on the cheek. "Just relax. If it helps, picture me in my underwear."

That image—Ricky lying on the bed, stretched out, nothing but golden skin and thin underwear that left little to the imagination—went straight to Darwin's cock. He groaned and tried to shift into a more comfortable position.

"There, see? Now you're not nervous anymore." Ricky waggled his eyebrows.

"You're a little shit," Darwin hissed.

"I've been called worse," he assured Darwin, smirking.

But his infectious grin seemed to have the desired effect as Darwin relaxed and leaned closer. The rest of the ride, Ricky chatted about his job hunting, his cat, and, happiest of all, how glad he was Darwin had called.

For his part, Darwin kept the conversation on Ricky. He didn't want to talk about himself. He couldn't be sure why, but Ricky finding out who he was frightened Darwin.

When the cab driver pulled up to the restaurant, Darwin gritted his teeth. They were really going to do this. They got out. Darwin paid for the cab then turned to the restaurant with its wide flower boxes, bursting with a variety of flowers in all the hues of the rainbow.

They entered the restaurant, and the host approached them. "Good evening, gentlemen. Welcome to Rossi's."

Darwin informed the host about their reservation. He'd asked Heather to make them, because he'd dined here before with clients and didn't want any fuss to ruin the night. She assured him it would be discreet.

The host showed them to a booth tucked away into the back corner. A red and white checked cloth covered the table, and a small oil lamp on one side illuminated the silk flowers.

"This looks wonderful," Ricky gushed as they sat.

The host handed them black leather-bound folders. Ricky opened his menu, and his eyes went wide.

"We are so in the wrong place," he whispered after the host had walked away.

Darwin cocked his head. "Why?"

"This menu doesn't even have prices."

The shock on Ricky's face made Darwin insanely happy. He'd never gone on a date with someone who would be concerned by cost. He and Dean had both had money when they'd met, and they'd never given a thought to buying a bottle of wine that might cost a few thousand dollars. He knew, without a doubt, Dean would have loved Ricky, too.

"That's because you have the date menu. You're not allowed to see the prices since I'm paying."

"Is it okay if I order a salad?"

"Don't you like the food? We can go somewhere else if you'd rather."

Ricky sighed. "It's not that. A meal at McDonald's is high cuisine for me. Plus, I can get a burger for Merlin. I worked in a restaurant like this, but other than the kitchen tastings, I've never eaten in one."

"Trust me, this place isn't like Asiago. The food is more comfort style, not... What did you call it? Pretentious. This is what you'd find in an Italian kitchen, made by an elderly grandmother who thinks you don't eat enough and wants to fatten you up so you'll settle down and get married."

Ricky's jaw dropped. "And you said *I* was a little shit."

"Please," Darwin said, "order whatever you want. It really isn't that expensive. If seeing the menu would make you feel better, I'll show you. I'd rather you didn't, because I don't want you to feel uncomfortable or anything. Just sit back and enjoy."

"No," Ricky said softly. He swallowed. "I guess if you can afford a shot of Macallan M, dinner shouldn't be a problem." As soon as he'd said the words, Ricky's eyes went wide. "Oh, damn. I'm sorry. I didn't mean it like that." He lowered his head to the tabletop. "Crap."

Taking Ricky's hand, Darwin smiled. "It's fine. I buy a shot once a year. I'm definitely not offended that you brought it up. And besides, it's nice you remembered me."

Ricky sat back up and stared at Darwin. "Well…it was kind of hard to forget you. You gave me one of the biggest tips I'd ever gotten there. For what you gave me, I'd have to work two full shifts. So thank you."

"You earned it, believe me. I treated you unfairly, and you didn't deserve that."

Holding up a hand, Ricky said, "Stop. Please. We've moved past that. You brought me in corn dogs and a shake. You tried to save me from being fired. I think you went well above any apology with that."

The thought warmed Darwin. "Okay, we won't talk about it again."

"So, what do you do for a living?"

And just like that, Darwin's mood crashed. He didn't want to answer, because until now, he'd truly been enjoying himself. But he also didn't want to lie, because he respected Ricky.

"I work in an office downtown." It was close enough to the truth.

"Okay, but doing what? I mean we talked about me, but I barely know anything about you. Favorite movies, music, books? Tell me about Darwin Kincade."

"Favorite movie: *Beetlejuice*. Favorite music: It's going to sound weird, but when I'm at home, I usually listen to classical. It relaxes me. But the music we danced to? That's my favorite. It reminds me of this great guy who took me out, got me drunk, and didn't take advantage of me."

The blush that stained Ricky's cheeks was absolutely adorable.

"I wouldn't, you know," Ricky said, averting his gaze.

"What?"

"Take advantage of you."

The earnestness in his voice, the blush on his cheeks, and look on his face told Darwin the story. It seemed important to Ricky that Darwin not think poorly of him. The arrival of the waiter saved him from having to comment.

"Good evening, gentlemen. My name is Simon, and I'll be serving you this evening. Would you like to start with a drink or an appetizer?"

Darwin looked at Ricky and arched his eyebrows.

Ricky put his menu down. "Nothing for me, thanks."

Darwin sighed. "We'll have a double Italian sampler platter and an order of seafood pockets. And to drink, a bottle of Pinot grigio, please."

The waiter jotted down the requests and told them he'd return in a few minutes to take their order. If Darwin thought he'd been nervous, now it seemed their positions had changed. Ricky kept sipping his water and looking anywhere but at Darwin.

"Ricky?" he said quietly, putting a hand over his date's as he again reached for his water.

"Yeah?"

"Please relax. I want this to be a fun date. Order anything you'd like. Try something you've never had before. If you like it, great. If not, we'll find something else. You showed me something new, so please let me do the same for you."

CHAPTER SIX

Ricky couldn't tear his gaze away from Darwin. He'd been on many dates, but they were usually with guys who took him somewhere cheap, and then expected him to put out at the end of it. Most of them had been disappointed, because Ricky didn't do casual sex. His parents had been married twenty-two years, and his mother had sat him down when he'd turned sixteen after he'd told them he was gay. She'd explained to him that she loved him and being gay was nothing to be ashamed of. She'd told him she still expected him to bring home a nice boy. One who respected and loved him. And in order to do that, he had to respect himself, and not simply sleep with someone for the sake of it. She'd said feelings were important, too. If he couldn't picture himself with a person in five, ten, twenty years, then maybe he needed to keep looking.

In his relationships, he'd always looked at the man to determine if he could see spending his life with them. He never told them, of course. No one wanted to hear that you were picturing them for the long haul on the first date. But Darwin? So very different. He had an innate kindness toward people—at least when he wasn't being prickly—and he said please and thank you to their server. That showed class and a good upbringing.

But what Ricky found most attractive turned out to be the way Darwin urged him to simply let go and enjoy himself. He could only recall a couple of guys who had said that, but it usually ended up with them splitting the bill. Darwin had said he wanted Ricky to have a good time, and he shouldn't worry about the cost. He did, though. Another life lesson from his mother. People who spent a lot of money on you generally expected something at the end of the meal. Like dessert, she'd said, waggling her brows.

Ricky didn't think Darwin would do that, though. He wasn't sure why, but he felt comfortable with the man. They'd only gone out once, but Darwin seemed to be looking for the same thing Ricky had been searching for. A true connection. Not a quick and easy lay. Ricky had already done that a few times and wound up hating himself the next morning.

When Simon returned with a bottle of Pinot grigio in a chilled ice bucket and a heaping plate of amazing smelling appetizers, Ricky sighed and picked up his menu again. When he'd seen the shrimp linguini listed on the menu as the evening special, his stomach rumbled. Fortunately, Darwin hadn't heard it. Or, if he had, he'd kept the fact to himself. The description sounded so good to Ricky—six shrimp in a garlic-parmesan sauce served over whole-wheat linguini. But still, he figured the salad would be cheaper. While the place might not be Asiago, Ricky had an inkling what the food cost.

"I'll have—"

"The shrimp linguini, right?" Darwin asked, a grin playing on his lips. "I saw your finger stop there for a bit. And the look on your face spoke volumes."

Ricky wanted to protest, but instead, he simply nodded.

"Excellent choice. We got the shrimp in today, and they're quite succulent. And you, sir?"

"I'd like the seafood combo, please. And if you wouldn't mind bringing a few extra plates, it would be appreciated."

"Of course. I'll return soon with your meals. In the meantime, I hope you enjoy your apps. If you need anything, please let me know."

"Thank you, Simon," Darwin said, handing the menus back to their server.

After he walked away, Ricky peered at Darwin. "Do you know how many people remember the names of their server?"

"Pretty few, I suppose."

"Like almost none. At Asiago, if people wanted my attention, they generally snapped their fingers at me like they were trying to call their dog. It's…nice to see someone who knows how to be decent to the help."

"Well, I'm glad. I have to go to the bathroom. Dig in and enjoy something while I'm gone. Since you're the professional, if you want to pour us a glass of wine, it would be appreciated."

Darwin stood and gave Ricky a smile.

"What?"

"Nothing," Darwin said, his eyes twinkling in the lamp light. "I'm really glad you're here."

With those words, he headed toward the back of the restaurant.

Dutifully, Ricky poured the wine, then placed a glass on Darwin's napkin. He chuckled, because the habit of setting a table had been so deeply engrained. The scent of the food had his stomach growling, so Ricky speared a toasted ravioli and dipped it in the warm marinara sauce. It practically melted in his mouth, and an embarrassing noise escaped.

"Good going," he mumbled. "Darwin's going to think you shouldn't be taken in public."

"How's the food?" Darwin asked, startling Ricky.

"I only tried the ravioli, but it's really good."

"Great. *Mangia!*"

Ricky cocked his head.

"It means eat in Italian. The owners are old-country trained. Their great-grandparents came over about sixty years ago and started this restaurant. It passed through the generations until Bertina and Gio took it over. And they'll be leaving it to their kids."

"Been here much?" Ricky teased.

Darwin grinned. "A couple times. I like the ambiance. These people? They make you feel like family." He paused a moment, then he cocked his head. "What would you think about working here?"

It wasn't as though the thought hadn't crossed his mind. From the little bit he'd seen, the relaxed atmosphere, the smiles of both the waitstaff and customers, plus the food? He knew he'd like this place. The problem, of course, it was too far from home to walk.

"I'd have to check the buses. The cab ride would cost me all the money I made on a good night."

Darwin opened his mouth, then closed it. He peered intently at Ricky, then said, "I think you'd be a great fit here. After what Louisa said about you at Asiago, it seems more your speed. Family is important to the owners, and they treat their staff right."

They chatted over the remainder of the appetizers, which Ricky couldn't stop eating. He kept telling himself he'd have just one more, but then Darwin would pick something up and put it on his plate, saying he had to try it. The more he tried, the more he could see himself waiting tables here.

When Simon brought out the main courses, Ricky gawped. Their plates were *loaded*.

"There's no way I can eat all this," Ricky said.

"We have to-go boxes," Simon told him, placing a small one beside Ricky.

"What's this?" he asked, opening the carton.

What he saw had him very confused.

"This is a piece of grilled salmon," Simon replied. Then he smiled at Ricky, gave Darwin a nod, and went to another table.

"But no one ordered it," Ricky protested.

"I did," Darwin admitted, gracing Ricky with a blush and an embarrassed smile.

"I don't understand."

Darwin scratched his cheek. "Okay, it sounds silly now, but I thought about your kitten at home, and figured he should get a doggy bag. When I went to the bathroom, I asked Simon to add it to our order."

"You...bought something for Merlin?"

His heart thumped wildly. Who went out on a date and bought something for a cat? He peered at Darwin and could see the pink in his cheeks deepen to scarlet.

"This is the nicest thing anyone has ever done for me," he whispered.

And it had been. Though he hadn't had Merlin long, the cat had become a friend to him, a confidante when he needed to share something and didn't think anyone would understand. He loved him as if he were the best buddy Ricky had. And to see Darwin care about him without an ulterior motive?

"Thank you," Ricky said, his voice choked with emotion.

"You're very welcome," Darwin replied, picking up his fork.

They ate in silence after that. Mostly because Ricky had no idea what to say. He kept looking over at the box of fish Darwin had gotten for Merlin, and no matter how many times he saw it, he couldn't accept that someone would go out of their way to do something like that.

"How's your dinner?" Darwin asked.

"I like this place," Ricky said around a mouthful of shrimp linguini. He took a sip of his Pinot grigio, then set his glass down.

"I'm glad. Do you want to try some of mine?"

"I'm good, thanks."

Darwin frowned, and Ricky found it to be the most adorable pout ever as his date's lower lip pushed out and quivered dramatically. "I got extra plates so we could try each other's dinners. Yours smells delicious. Even if you don't want to try mine, I want to taste yours."

A laugh bubbled out of Ricky at the expression on Darwin's face. "Okay, I'd like to try your scallops, if you don't mind. I've never had them before."

Darwin heaped the side plate full of things from his entree, and Ricky grinned.

"I don't think all of those are scallops," he teased.

"No, but they're all so good. I wanted to share."

As Ricky popped a breaded scallop into his mouth, he glanced over at Darwin, whose smile made him feel warm on the inside. His mother's words drifted back to him once more. Though this had

75

been their first real date and they had so much to learn about one another, he could see making a home with Darwin. Raising a family. Darwin was the one person he'd been out with that his mother would be proud of. Maybe he should talk to her. But then she'd want to meet him, and wouldn't that just be awkward?

****

Darwin had to force himself to look at his plate. His gaze kept drifting toward Ricky and the wide green eyes that seemed to be taking everything in. They'd finished their dinner and sat eating a bowlful of spumoni ice cream and drinking a cup of coffee.

"Did you like your dinner?"

"Oh my God, I'm so stuffed. I may not have to eat again all week. Everything was so good, but I really loved the pasta. Thank you for encouraging me to get it."

"I'm glad. I wanted you to enjoy yourself. I liked seeing it."

"So are you ready to put aside the elephant in the room?" Ricky asked, pinning Darwin with a stare.

Darwin froze. He couldn't imagine what Ricky meant. Did he know who Darwin was? Or had he been talking about something else?

"I'm not sure what you mean."

"Well, every time I try to ask you a question about yourself, you hedge. You turn the conversation back to me. I'd really like to get to know you."

It took Darwin a few seconds to calm himself. He pushed his ice cream aside, folded his arms on the table, and met Ricky's gaze.

Darwin took a deep breath, mentally preparing himself for what would likely be a difficult conversation. "What would you like to know?"

"Really? So I can ask you anything?"

Darwin narrowed his eyes. "Well, I don't know about *anything*, but I'll do my best to answer anything you ask."

"Siblings?"

"One. My older brother, Kent."

"Parents?"

"Yes," Darwin replied, trying to give Ricky what Henley called Darwin's infuriating smirk.

Ricky cocked his head. "Yes?"

"Well, I'm assuming you're asking if I have them." Darwin grinned.

Ricky groaned and rolled his eyes. "Okay, you got me there."

"In answer to your question, they died a long time ago."

"Oh. I'm sorry. My dad died, too. My mom really misses him. Me and my sister do, too."

Reaching out to hold Ricky's hand, Darwin realized how much he enjoyed this. Conversation. Touching. Just being with someone. Sure, he'd had his fantasies about Roy, but Ricky was flesh and blood, warm and alive. He stroked his fingers over the back of Ricky's hand, and when he saw the goose bumps, it sent a little jolt through him.

"Nothing to be sorry for, I promise." Darwin detected Ricky's sadness, so he decided to go back to safe topics. "So you've got to tell me. How did you end up at Asiago?"

Ricky grinned. "Would you believe dumb luck? I'd had a few other jobs in restaurants, and I enjoyed them for the most part. But those types of places really didn't pay the bills. I started putting in applications in other places and decided to stop at Asiago. Their ad said they wanted someone with five years serving experience. All combined, I did have five years, but not in the type of dining they did. When Louisa saw my resume, her eyebrows disappeared into her hairline. She started to say something, probably that I didn't have the experience, but then she got a call off. She was furious, because it wasn't the guy's first time saying he was sick. She fired him and hired me on the spot."

The cheeky grin he got had Darwin laughing. When Simon slid the check folder onto the table, Darwin snatched it up, wanting to keep Ricky from snooping. He glanced at the bill, wrote in a three-hundred-dollar tip, and slipped it back to Simon. When he went to the register, he heard the cashier gasp and look over at them, a hand covering her mouth. Darwin gave her a nod. A few moments later, Simon came back to the table, a very wide smile on his face.

"Thank you so much, gentlemen. I hope you have a very pleasant evening." Then he strode away, looking very much like he was on cloud nine.

Darwin grinned and put his credit card in his wallet, then slipped his billfold back into his pocket. He turned to Ricky, his smile lingering, and said, "So, what should we do?"

A slight frown crossed Ricky's face. "I should go home. I have to feed Merlin, plus I need to hit the streets again tomorrow. Jobs aren't easy to come by. Since I was only at Asiago for a few months, it really doesn't look good on my resume. I know Louisa said she'd give me a glowing recommendation, but I'm guessing people see the fact I quit, and that's it for me."

I'll get you a job. Tell me what you want to do. The words were on the tip of Darwin's tongue. Hell, if Ricky wanted, Darwin would *buy* Asiago for him. But Ricky wasn't the kind of guy you threw money at. His reaction to the piece of fish for his cat had proven that. And Darwin didn't want to start their relationship in that way. He wanted Ricky to like him for who he was.

"Apply here," he said brightly. "What's the worst that could happen?"

"I'm thinking about it," Ricky replied. He rubbed the back of his neck. "Would you mind if we called it a night?"

"Yes. I really would," Darwin answered truthfully. "But I know why, and it's important, so I'll ask them to get us a cab."

Ricky's smile lit up Darwin's heart. It could never be seen as anything less than genuine. Just like the man himself. He waved at the host, and asked if he'd mind calling for them. He said he'd be delighted and headed back to the desk. Ricky stood, picked up his boxes of food, and they left the restaurant.

The night air had finally cooled off some. No longer sweltering, it provided a welcome respite from the heat they'd been crushed by for the last week. He sat on the bench outside, and Darwin smiled when Ricky took the spot next to him.

"I had a really nice time. Thank you."

Darwin dipped his chin. "Me, too. Thank you for coming with me."

They sat in companionable silence for a few minutes. Then Darwin jumped when Ricky took his hand and laced their fingers together.

"Sorry," Ricky said, pulling his hand back. "I should have asked if you were out. I don't want to cause you any problems."

The loss of connection speared Darwin. He couldn't believe how much he missed it already. *What are you doing to me? Is it because I've been so lonely? No. I can't believe that. Since you spoke up at Asiago, you've been on my mind. Why do I react to you the way I do?*

"No, no. Definitely out. It just surprised me is all. Could I...?"

He held out his hand, and joy surged through him when Ricky slipped his hand into Darwin's. The biggest surprise came when Ricky leaned over and rested his head on Darwin's shoulder.

"I really don't want this night to end," Ricky admitted, then sighed. "Everything was...perfect. Especially the company."

Darwin tilted his head until it touched Ricky's. He could smell a lemony scent, likely his shampoo or body wash, sharp and tangy. It would be forever linked in his mind with Ricky. He'd give anything to freeze this moment in time.

"For me, too. I can't believe how nervous I was about calling you."

"Ha! I hoped you would, but if I'm honest, I was equally nervous. I don't really date much, so I wasn't sure what the proper protocol is."

"None," Darwin insisted. "You have my number. If you ever want to call me, regardless of the reason, do it." He was quiet for a minute, then Ricky shuffled a little closer. "I'd like to see you again. Would that be okay?"

Ricky squeezed Darwin's hand. "Gee, I don't know."

The light, teasing tone, coupled with the warmth of Ricky's hand gave Darwin a sense of peace. They sat there, not saying anything until the cab pulled up.

The whole ride back to Ricky's apartment, he stayed pressed up against Darwin, as if taking comfort in his presence. Darwin had no complaints at all. The interior of the cab smelled of the food in Ricky's to-go boxes, a rich, delicious scent that had Darwin's stomach rumbling.

"Want to take some of this home?" Ricky asked, chuckling.

"No. If I get hungry—" He stopped. He'd almost said his cook would warm him up some cabbage rolls. "I'm pretty sure there are some pizza rolls in the freezer." Another thing he'd never tried, but if Henley hadn't left him any of Maria's specialty, maybe he'd indulge himself tonight and eat something from his friend's stash.

"Those won't make a meal for you. I've still got two containers of linguini. Take one."

He picked one up and held it out toward Darwin. He thought about taking it without arguing, but this could be a couple of meals for Ricky, and probably Merlin, too. Ricky needed it more than Darwin.

"No, I'm good. Thanks. Shouldn't even be hungry. I think it's the smell of the food that's triggering the *Feed Me, Seymour* vibe."

"You like *Little Shop of Horrors*? I loved the one with Rick Moranis. He was absolutely adorable in that role," Ricky said with a chuckle.

"I liked Levi Stubbs as Audrey II. He had an incredible singing voice."

Ricky opened his mouth, then closed it as the cab pulled up in front of his apartment. A strange loneliness swept through Darwin. He didn't want the night to be over. He wanted... He wanted to sit on the couch with Ricky. Share their favorite movies. Anything to not have to go home to a big, empty house.

"Can I walk you in?" he asked, trying to hide the sadness.

"I'd like that."

They got out of the cab. Darwin stuck his head into the open window and asked the driver if he'd mind waiting a few minutes. The man seemed ready to protest when Darwin flashed him a one-hundred-dollar bill.

"No problem at all, sir!" the driver said with a little too much enthusiasm.

Darwin walked Ricky into the vestibule of his apartment. They stood for a moment, simply staring into each other's eyes. Then Ricky put his hand on the back of Darwin's neck and pulled him down into a kiss. It wasn't anything like the one the night at the bar. This one screamed need and desire as Ricky's tongue probed Darwin's mouth, licking, teasing, ratcheting up the desire. When he stepped back, Darwin felt the loss immediately.

"Good night," Ricky whispered, then rushed to the elevator.

He wanted to call after Ricky. Ask him if he could come up. Maybe meet Merlin or have an after-dinner drink. He hesitated, because he'd seen the widened pupils, the desire in Ricky's eyes. If Ricky allowed him to come upstairs, he wouldn't want to leave.

Darwin watched for a few moments after the doors closed and the elevator whisked Ricky away before he returned to the cab and asked the driver to take him home.

CHAPTER SEVEN

Ricky closed the door as soon as he got into his apartment. Merlin lay on the couch and glared at Ricky when he walked in.

"Oh, don't look at me like that," Ricky groused. "I got something special for you, but if you're going to be like that, you won't get it."

Merlin bounded off the couch and rushed to follow Ricky into the kitchen.

"Yeah, thought that might get your attention." He blew a raspberry at the cat. "You know you're going to have to listen when I tell you about dinner, right? I had the *best* time. He's sweet, charming, and has a quirky sense of humor. And after I put everything away, I'll give you what he spent good money on to make you happy."

After packing the leftovers into the refrigerator, with Merlin's loud whines chastising him, Ricky took half of the salmon, chopped it up, and put it into a bowl for the kitten. Apparently all was forgiven when he dove into the dish.

"I almost asked him to spend the night," Ricky told his cat.

Ricky walked across the room and slumped onto his chair, going over the thoughts he'd had in the lobby. He'd *never* asked anyone to stay. On the rare occasions he'd gone home with someone, it had always been to their place, and Ricky always left right after. Until tonight, there hadn't been anyone who he would ask to stay.

Darwin had thrown himself into the kiss as though he'd been starving. He'd sucked Ricky's tongue while holding him tightly. No way could Ricky have missed the need pulsing through the man. When he'd stepped back, he could see desire and a hint of sadness in

Darwin's gaze. Ricky knew he had to get to his apartment before he asked for something he wasn't sure they were ready for.

With shaky hands, he extracted his phone and dialed his sister.

"Do you know what time it is?" she snapped.

"Um. No, not really. Sorry."

Her voice softened when she asked, "You okay?"

He wasn't sure. He thought he was, but right now he missed Darwin. His touch. His very presence.

"I dunno." He sniffled. "I'm sorry. I shouldn't have called. We'll talk later."

"Don't you dare hang up that phone, Richard!" she snapped. "Talk to me. You really wouldn't want to make me call Mom."

He snorted. His mom would be far worse. A dog with a bone had nothing on the woman.

"I sort of went out on a date tonight," he admitted.

"And that's a bad thing?"

"I wanted to ask him to stay." When she didn't reply, he asked, "Trish?"

"I'm sorry. I just can't... You wanted to ask a man to stay with you?"

"I know, right?" he replied, watching Merlin lick his lips at his treat. "How messed up is that?"

"I take it you like this guy? Tell me about him."

And he did—from their initial meeting, to their night at the bar, to this date, he told her everything. When he finished, she sighed.

"Oh, Ricky. That's the most precious thing I've ever heard. We're talking Oprah's women's network level romance. He bought food for your cat." She sighed again.

"Really? Out of that entire story, you latch onto the salmon he bought?"

"I'm sorry," she replied. "Jack used to do sweet things when we were dating. Flowers, little gifts, the whole ball of wax. Then after we got married, he seemed to think it wasn't necessary anymore. The last time we had a romantic dinner was when we were at Golden Chicken with the kids."

"How in the hell is that romantic?"

Trish laughed. "They had a small fire in the kitchen. It reminded me of a fireplace, so I took it as a bit of romance. Don't harsh my mellow."

Ricky chuckled. Only his sister would take meaning from a kitchen fire.

"Do you like him?" she asked quietly.

"That's the weird thing. I really, *really* do," he replied. "But it's only been like one and a half dates."

"Did Mom ever tell you about her first date with dad?"

Ricky thought back. "No."

"Okay, do me a favor and call her. You're going to want to hear what she has to say."

"But it's Mom," he whined.

"Who will kick your ass if she finds out what you just did," she teased. Then her voice softened. "Trust me on this one. Call her now."

"It's late," he reminded her.

"I know, but Mom needs to hear about your new man, and you need to hear her story. Call me tomorrow."

She hung up. Ricky ran a thumb over the screen on his phone. When he saw his mother's number, he hesitantly dialed.

"Are you sick? In the hospital? Need blood?"

"Mom." He huffed. "What are you talking about?"

"Well, you're calling. I figure something must be wrong."

He realized he hadn't talked to her for a few weeks and his stomach tightened. "Sorry. Things have been pretty hectic here. I quit my job before I got fired."

"Are you okay? Do you need anything?"

He loved his mother. They were no longer kids, but she would do anything for him and his sister. "I'm fine. Listen, Trish told me to call you and ask about your first date with dad."

"Have you met someone?"

He refused to commit to an answer. "Maybe."

"I'm glad," she replied. "We'll be talking about him, you know. And I want to meet him!"

"I figured as much."

"What's wrong with him?"

"Oh, God. Not one damn thing that I've seen so far." He retold the tale of Darwin, from their first encounter at the restaurant, to the dinner they'd shared tonight. Afterward, like his sister, she sighed.

"He sounds delightful."

"He is. So about this first date?"

"Impatient brat. You must get that from your father, because no one on my side of the family is like that."

Ricky choked back a laugh. He loved his mother, but there were plenty of times when they were growing up, she would ask something, then she would demand to know why they hesitated with an answer if you didn't tell her what she wanted to hear within five seconds of the question.

"Okay, so let me set the scene for you. We were supposed to go out on our first date that afternoon and see the fireworks that evening. We were going to do a picnic in the park, and then walk over to see the display. I'd never looked forward to anything more in my life."

And Ricky knew that to be the truth. Before Kyle Connelly died, he'd been hopelessly devoted to his wife and children. His father had become the man that Ricky measured all others against. He could easily see the attraction his mother spoke of.

"It had rained early on, and the weather had gotten cool. That morning, I woke up, pulled out my dress so I could be sure it wasn't wrinkled, then set to making sure everything was perfect. Of course this is the point in the story where everything goes to hell."

"What happened?" Ricky asked, now needing to hear the story.

"You know what the problem is with your generation? You have no sense of dramatic flair. Anyway, Mom got a call from Grandma

Beth, saying they were taking Grandpa Hank to the hospital. She told me I'd need to stay home and watch Ellen and Maggie. I protested, for all the good it did. I'd waited weeks for this day, and now she wanted me to take care of my sisters? I complained about how unfair it all was, but in the end, I called your father and broke our date."

Ricky slumped into his chair. Obviously the story had a happy ending, but he could feel the heartbreak in her softly spoken words.

"I was angry, because it had taken him weeks to get up the nerve to ask me. I almost went to him, because he was sweet and charming and I had found myself smitten."

"Smitten?" Ricky teased.

"It's a perfectly nice word," she swore. "Anyway, about four o'clock, the doorbell rang. I opened it, and there he stood. He had on a dark blue suit with a thin red tie that had gold stripes on it, and he wore polished loafers. He was, without a doubt, the most beautiful thing I'd ever seen.

"I asked him why he had come when I'd canceled, and he said if he didn't, he couldn't be sure he'd have the nerve to ask again. He brought a picnic lunch. When I reminded him I had to watch your aunts, he assured me he had enough food for all of us. He invited me out to the picnic table in our backyard, where he'd already set up the food. We all took a seat. It didn't matter to him that we were effectively babysitting because, he said, family always came first. In fact, he treated my sisters better than I had. He made sure they had enough food, that they weren't cold, and he played games with them when they complained they were bored. I cried a little at that.

"If you asked me today, I couldn't tell you for sure what we ate. I just know that it had been the most romantic gesture I'd ever seen."

Ricky's heart stuttered. His whole family missed his father. The man had always been generous with his hugs, his praise, and his time. His heart attack at forty had devastated their family, and it had taken years for them to get back to a semblance of normal.

"That's why I ask you to see if you can picture yourself having a future with someone. That afternoon, sitting outside with your dad, my whole life laid itself out before my eyes. I knew that one day we'd be married. Six months later, he actually proposed. I said yes, of course."

He'd never heard the story, and the sweetness of her words brought a burning to his eyes. He knew how much she loved their father. She'd never remarried, telling them that no one could ever take his place. She'd gone out on dates, but never felt that connection with anyone.

"Thank you for telling me," he said, his voice cracking.

"Can you picture being with this man? Does he make your toes curl? Make your heart sing? If you look at him now, can you see yourself in twenty years, sitting across from him, sipping coffee? This is what love is, honey. It's not whether you're compatible in bed, but if you can be in life."

Ricky didn't even have to consider her question. It had been on his mind since their date. "Yeah, Mom. I can. I sat with him at dinner and found myself wondering what it would be like for us to be in our kitchen, making a meal for our family. Working together to create something beautiful."

"Yes!" she said, practically shouting. "That's how I felt with your dad. Hold on to that feeling. Remember it, because when things go wrong—and they always do—it's that which will keep you together. Problems come and go, but if you're together, love can always see you through the worst of times."

When his phone beeped, Ricky pulled it away from his ear, smiling when he saw who the caller was.

"Mom? Darwin's calling. Can I call you back?"

"Anytime. Go talk to your man."

He connected with Darwin and had to suppress a sigh when he heard the breathy tone in Darwin's voice.

"I was wondering…are you doing anything this weekend?"

"Probably filling out more applications. Why?"

"What would you say if I asked whether you wanted to take a ride down by the lake? See the sights. Maybe do a little exploring."

Ricky didn't even have to think about it. "Yes, that would be really nice."

"I'll call you later and we can confirm plans. Sound okay?"

"Sounds great," Ricky replied, butterflies in his stomach multiplying at the thought of another date with Darwin. "Are you home yet?"

"Just pulling up. Thank you again for tonight. Sleep well."

****

Darwin put his phone back into his pocket. He hadn't even been away from Ricky for half an hour, and he already missed him. His warmth, and that kiss that sent tingles through his body. He couldn't believe how much Ricky had come to mean to him in such a short time.

After he paid the driver, including the hundred dollars he'd offered, Darwin let himself into the house. Compared to Ricky's building, the place seemed cold. He'd never really liked living there, even as a child. When there'd been a full staff, it was filled with people, but they never had time to do anything but work. Even his nanny had needed to fulfill other responsibilities.

It had been different when Dean moved in. The house had been filled with love and the whole dynamic of the place changed. The servants had been invited to dine with him and Dean to get to know one another, to become part of the household. Hell, they'd become his and Dean's family. Then after Dean had died, Darwin couldn't stand to see their home anymore. He'd thought about moving, but this had been his only tie to his parents, his brother, and the man he'd loved with his whole heart.

A light in the kitchen let him know someone, probably Henley, could be caught raiding the refrigerator. He snuck in as quiet as he could and stood there while the man loaded up a plate with cabbage rolls.

"Don't think I don't know you're there, Dare. You're not the ninja type. Want some?"

"You mean there are still leftovers? Judging from the mound on that plate, I figured you'd have eaten them all by now."

"Funny. Ha. Yeah. She made extra, figuring you might want a snack before bed."

"So you're eating my snack?"

Henley closed the door and dropped his bounty on the counter. He licked his fingers. "You snooze, you lose, bud. You know how it goes."

Darwin reached out and snatched one off the plate, grabbed his own dish from the cabinet, and cut into it. Even cold they were amazing.

"How'd it go? You're home earlier than I figured," Henley said, popping his plate into the microwave.

"He's going job hunting again tomorrow. And he had to get home to feed his cat."

"Um. You hate cats."

Not entirely true. He'd never had pets growing up. His parents had told him he'd need to wait until he was older, because he had to learn responsibility first. He didn't find out until much later why his parents didn't allow animals in the house.

"I don't know cats. Except for the guard dogs that they used to have, I don't even know dogs."

Henley took his plate from the microwave, placed it on the table, and sliced into a cabbage roll, then glared at Darwin. "You know how much I loved living here, but honestly? Your parents were too uptight. Kids are supposed to get messy. They're supposed to have pets to play with."

"Yeah, well, it's hard to have the governor in your home when you're worried that Muffy or Tiffy will jump all over him," Darwin replied. "They told me when I turned eighteen the real reason. Appearances and all that."

"Not sure I could live like that," Henley admitted.

"Well, you could have a dog now. Why don't you?"

Henley shrugged. "I'm not home enough. If we're not out on the road, then I'm out at the bar."

Henley didn't really go to the bar that often, but he liked using it as an excuse. Darwin knew his friend needed someone in his life, but he also knew it had to be a very special person to catch the attention of Henley Davidson.

"So, how was the night?"

"Honestly? It was amazing. Dinner was delicious, but the company? That made the night perfect. And when we got home, he gave me a kiss that nearly melted me."

Henley made a pained noise. When Darwin looked up, his friend smiled. "Sorry, swallowed wrong."

"I'm going to take him for a drive this weekend," Darwin said. "We'll head down Lake Drive and check out some of the houses and also enjoy the view of the water."

Henley gaped at him. "Who's driving?"

Darwin sighed. "I am."

"That's funny," Henley said, but he wasn't laughing. In fact, he actually looked a little angry. "I've been your driver since you were eighteen. I don't know that you've ever even been behind the wheel. If you want to go, I'll take you."

A moment of panic gripped Darwin. "No, that's fine. I've got my license, even if I don't use it. I'm going to rent a car for the day, so there's no need."

"You think I don't know what this is about, right?"

"What do you mean?" Darwin asked, trying not to show his discomfort.

"He doesn't know who you are, does he?"

"Sure, he does."

"No," Henley corrected. "He knows the man who ate in his section at a restaurant. The one who brought corn dogs in so they could have dinner. He doesn't know the man who could call his pilot and have the private jet fly them to Paris for a midnight snack, and then hop over to Australia to watch the sunrise. What's up with that?"

The concern in Henley's expression loosened some of the guilt Darwin had been carrying around. "It's not like I want to deceive him," he said. "But I want him to like *me*, not who the money supposedly makes me."

Before he'd met Dean, he'd been asked on a couple of dates. He'd turned them down, because the men had been so transparent. Darwin had seen the dollar signs in their eyes. They hadn't wanted him, only the money and prestige that were part and parcel of being with him.

"And you don't trust him enough to do that? Has he given you any indication he would like you less?"

Darwin chose his words carefully, wanting Henley to understand his reasoning. "I bought some Macallan M when I had dinner that night. He gasped, literally, when I told him what I wanted. He tried to tell me how much it cost, and I told him I knew the price. Then apologized for my behavior, which had been atrocious. He forgave me, then teased me about my attitude. So the waters started out choppy, then calmed to the point where he teased me, made me feel...better.

"After that, it had been corn dogs and shakes, him buying me drinks at a bar and dancing the night away. Window-shopping in stores he said he'd never be able to buy from, but he liked looking at the fancy things. Money isn't him. And I don't want him to look at me differently."

Henley put a hand on Darwin's shoulder and gave a slight squeeze. "So you'd rather lie to him. Pretend to be something you're not. I can see that being the basis of a good relationship."

"You don't understand..." Darwin protested. He really needed Henley to see what he meant. He wasn't sure why it was so important, but Darwin needed his friend's blessing.

"No, I don't. And you're not explaining it very well either. You want to keep him in the dark, pretend with him. What if it turns serious? Do you really think you can keep this a secret? How long before he finds out?" Henley paused a moment, took a bite, then started again. "Seriously, Dare, it's not like your face isn't on the financial pages often enough. What's he going to think when he sees that the guy he's been going out with has more money that God?"

"I don't have that much money," Darwin replied, hating the whine in his voice.

Henley snorted. "You were one of the richest men under thirty-five for the last four years. Pretty soon you'll be on the list for under forty. How much money do you think that takes?"

"Why are you being like this?' Darwin demanded.

Henley sighed. "Because I'm your friend, Dare. The one person who is always going to be honest with you. If you care for him, and I mean really care, you'll trust him and tell him the truth. Because if you can't, then you obviously don't have true feelings for him and are only interested in the situation." He picked up his plate. "Let me know if you need to go anywhere. I'm going to my room to watch some television."

Darwin stood as Henley's footsteps echoed down the hall.

"Why does he have to be so…" Darwin sighed. "Right."

He'd needed to hear it, he knew. The thought scared him to death, though. Darwin rarely felt comfortable with people. Only special people could slip under his defenses, and Ricky definitely qualified. But he wasn't being fair to the man. A lie of omission still counted as a lie. He finished his cabbage roll, rinsed off the plate, and slipped it into the dishwasher. Then he sucked in a deep breath and went down the hall to Henley's room.

His friend didn't get angry often, but he could hold a grudge over stupid things at times. Darwin hesitated for a moment before he knocked. He breathed a sigh of relief when Henley told him to come in.

"Figured you'd be here soon," he said, polishing off the last of his cabbage rolls. He pointed at his plate, then asked, "You didn't bring any more, did you?"

Darwin laughed. Henley usually ate healthy meals, but when Maria made her specialty, all bets went out the window.

"No, sorry." Darwin pointed to the chair at the desk. "Can I sit?

Henley nodded, and Darwin pulled out the chair. He glanced around his friend's room. Auto magazines were piled in a neat stack on the desk, and his Mac had tabs open on fixing cars. He loved that the man took such great pride in his work, and that it carried over into his own passions.

"You were right," Darwin admitted. "I'm afraid. How do you tell someone you're rich, especially when they don't have anything?"

"You look him in the eye, and say, 'hey, just so you know, I've got money.'"

Darwin huffed and glared at his friend. "Can you be serious?"

"I am. Maybe you'll be less blunt, but there really isn't a way to break it gently."

"And what do I do if he gets angry?" Darwin fisted his hair. "I've never had to do this before, damn it. Dean had money. He knew the kind of life we have. Ricky told me his idea of high cuisine is eating a Big Mac."

"Okay, let me ask you something. Do you think the man is worth it?"

Darwin thought for a moment. "Is it okay if I say I really want him to be?"

Henley smiled. "Yeah, that's perfect."

CHAPTER EIGHT

The week crawled by for Ricky. He'd figured out the bus routes he'd need to get to Rossi's. A sense of relief flooded him when he discovered it would only be two busses, and that the travel time wouldn't be as long as he'd feared.

He applied on Tuesday afternoon and was delighted to hear back from Bertina Rossi Wednesday morning. She'd invited him in for an interview. When he sat down, she offered him a glass of water, which he declined. An older woman with the deepest laugh lines Ricky had ever seen, she had her gray hair pulled back into a bun. Ricky could tell from the gleam in her eye she definitely wasn't matronly. In fact, he imagined she had quite a devilish streak in her.

"Why do you want to work here, Richard?" she asked, giving him a smile that soothed the butterflies. This had been the first callback he'd gotten, and things were getting a little tight. He *really* needed to ace this interview.

"Well, we had dinner here on Monday. I like the atmosphere, and the food was absolutely delicious. When I looked around, I saw the customers and they seemed to really enjoy the place. I want to be a part of that. I like making people happy, and I think I could be a good fit here."

She tapped her pen on the desk and hummed. "I'll be honest. I love your application, but I'm a little concerned over your job at Asiago. You didn't stay there very long. May I ask why?"

Ricky hedged. It would be bad form to talk about a former employer in an unflattering way. "I hope you don't mind, but I'm not really comfortable explaining that. If you speak to the manager at

Asiago—Louisa—she said she would give me a good reference. I just feel it wouldn't be right for me to talk about my former employers in a way that may portray them in anything less than a fair light."

Bertina stood, and Ricky's heart slumped. Yet another job he wouldn't be getting. He got up and held out his hand.

"I appreciate your time."

She took his hand in hers and held him there for a moment. "Thank you for coming. Would you be available to start training on Monday?"

At first, he thought he heard wrong. "I'm sorry, what?"

She laughed, and it reminded him of his grandmother. A deep, rich alto—the kind that read the best bedtime stories. "If you want the job, it's yours. Can you start Monday?"

"Yes, ma'am."

"There are no ma'ams here. You can call me Bertie. Welcome to Rossi's."

She gave him copies of the menu for both lunch and dinner, a list of drinks available from the bar, and an employee packet that explained responsibilities, side work, breaks, free meals, hours, and many other things. For a family run restaurant, it seemed a lot more thorough than Asiago had been.

"Thank you, Bertie. I really appreciate the chance," he told her truthfully.

"So you know, I already talked to Louisa. I honestly did like your application. In fact, the job was yours before you walked in the door. But Louisa told me what happened had nothing to do with you, even if she wouldn't go into detail. She spoke about you in glowing terms. I just wanted to see what you'd tell me. I admire loyalty, Richard. Even when a job screwed you over, you still didn't need to sink to their level. That's class."

Ricky's cheeks grew warm at the unexpected praise.

"Besides, I know Gregory Berkhardt. I've got no problem believing everything was his fault," she said, giving him a knowing look. "His loss will definitely be our gain. We're looking forward to Monday, Richard."

"Please, call me Ricky."

"All right then. See you soon...Ricky."

They shook hands again, and he walked out into the too hot afternoon. He had a job. What's more, he had a job that seemed tailor made for him. He couldn't wait to tell his mom and Trish. Darwin would flip when... Darwin.

He drew in a deep breath. Funny how, when he had news to share, Darwin came to mind right away.

He made his phone calls to Mom and Trish when he got home, secure in the overworked AC's life-giving coolness. They were over the moon for him, but oddly enough, they wanted to talk more about Darwin. Ricky had no problems doing that.

After they talked, he thought about calling Darwin to tell him about the job, but he hesitated. He wanted to see him in person. To hug him when he gave him the news. He gave thought to calling him and inviting him out, but he'd stretched his finances pretty close to the breaking point. He'd split the leftover food from their dinner into meals and frozen it so that he wouldn't have to buy groceries. He wouldn't get a paycheck for a few weeks, and who knew how much he'd actually make in tips? But still, he had a job. Something solid to hold onto, and that would get him through this tough time.

He finally decided he would tell Darwin on their date. Though he'd probably crack long before then. But Darwin had encouraged him to apply, so Ricky knew he'd be almost as excited. If everything worked out, when they went on dates in the future, Ricky could afford to pay for things, too.

He didn't talk to Darwin until Friday afternoon. He called to see if Ricky still wanted to go for the drive on Saturday morning.

"Of course. I've been looking forward to it. And I've got something to tell you!"

Darwin seemed subdued when he replied he, too, had something he needed to talk about.

"Everything okay?"

Ricky didn't believe it when Darwin said, "Sure. All good. I'll pick you up tomorrow at nine. Will that be okay?"

"Yes, it will be. Are we going to stop for lunch?"

A voice in the background called for Mr. Kincade, and Darwin sighed. "I've got to go. Yes, we can stop for lunch. There are a few nice places along the way, but not ones where you'd need to get dressed up. Sound good?"

"Perfect. I'll see you tomorrow then."

He disconnected the call, then spent the afternoon reading over the paperwork Bertie had given him and playing with Merlin. He had a good feeling about the upcoming drive with Darwin.

****

"It's been a while, Dare. Are you sure you remember how to do this?"

Darwin stuck out his tongue and put the car in reverse. He backed out of the long, circular drive and put the car in gear.

"See, no problem."

Driving the car had been more challenging than he'd expected. He hadn't driven himself since he'd turned eighteen. Henley had taken him everywhere, or if Darwin needed some alone time, he'd caught a cab. Now they were doing a refresher course at Henley's insistence. He had to admit life definitely seemed different when you were the one behind the wheel.

Nerves continued to ratchet up as Henley directed them into more populous areas. Traffic in Chicago had him clutching the damn wheel for life. How the hell did Henley do this on a daily basis? Yet his friend seemed oddly comfortable as the passenger, and Darwin took that as high praise.

He relaxed slightly as he got more used to the ebb and flow of the traffic around them. Only twice did he have to slam on the brakes, and then listen to Henley's reminder about Chicago drivers and their definite lack of patience. Still, by the time they returned home, Henley seemed happy with Darwin's progress.

"You did good, Dare. Not sure you should be driving the two of you, though."

"We'll be okay," he promised as they stepped into the great room. "No breaking the speed limit, no cutting people off. Just like you taught me. And, Henley? Thank you. I couldn't have done this without your help."

He hugged his friend, taking comfort in the familiar embrace. How many times had Henley been there for him after Dean had died? Darwin doubted he could count that high. The man had always been at Darwin's side, ready to do whatever needed doing. He'd encourage Darwin when the hard feelings hit him, or he'd kick his ass when Darwin felt sorry for himself.

"Have you decided what you're going to do?" Henley asked.

Darwin knew what he meant. They hadn't discussed whether Darwin planned to tell Ricky the truth about himself on this drive.

"I'm going to tell him. I want to do it somewhere quiet. I'm scared to death, though," Darwin admitted.

Henley sat in one of the overstuffed armchairs near the fireplace, while Darwin took the sofa. When his friend leaned forward, elbows on his knees, Darwin knew the conversation had only just begun.

"If he can't handle being with you, then maybe you're better off. You shouldn't have to hide who you are for people to like you."

The words stung, but they were the truth. As much as he enjoyed spending time with Ricky, if he couldn't accept who he had been dating, then it would be best to break it off now, before feelings got too deep, and it hurt more.

The problem? It would devastate him. He wasn't ready to put a label on his feelings, but they were already strong. Not talking to Ricky this week had left him fidgety. He'd wanted to drive over to his apartment and whisk him away for a romantic evening. The honest truth, which he would only tell himself, he wanted to give Ricky everything. He'd never had a reaction this strong. Even when he'd been with Dean, their feelings had started out as friendship and grown into love.

Love.

Darwin knew the truth. Without a doubt, he found himself head over heels in love with Ricky. Yeah, it had only been a very short time, but after losing Dean, he realized how life had no guarantees. If Darwin wanted something, he needed to admit it. And he did want Ricky. Not just in bed, but beside him for the long haul.

"You really care for him, don't you?" Henley asked.

Darwin nodded.

"I'm glad, Dare," he said as he got up, sat next to Darwin, and pulled him into an embrace. "I haven't seen you like this in far too long. It really is a good look on you."

"What do you mean?"

Henley sat back, not breaking their connection, and gave him a sad smile. "You think I don't know you? We've shared far too much throughout the years. I remember the look on your face when you realized what Dean meant to you. It took both of you long enough to admit you wanted each other. I know it started out as friendship, but I watched when the two of you would be at the same functions. I could feel the electricity from the back of the room. I knew you were meant to be together.

"When he moved in, your whole life revolved around him. All of us saw the change in you. Where before you'd been more like your parents—cold and aloof—you became warm and caring. We loved seeing the two of you in love. It brought a warmth that the house had never had. And when he died...we all grieved with you. You might have been our employer, but you were family, too. We hated seeing you crumble in on yourself. And we really missed the sunshine."

Darwin couldn't stop the tears. They streamed down his cheeks, and Henley hugged him harder.

"Let it out. I don't think you ever really did."

Another truth. He'd cried for his loss when Dean died, but all the hurt and anger at himself for not being there and for the disease that took Dean away knotted up inside him. The thought he couldn't give his heart to anyone else, because it would be too easy to break. He'd lost himself in his work for years, not accepting invitations to parties, making only cursory visits to company affairs, because he'd feared putting himself out there again. Then Ricky had come into his life, and Darwin knew he'd wasted too much time on what might happen.

Henley held him for hours as all the pain and rage seeped out of him, replaced with a calm he hadn't experienced in such a long time. When he finally drew back, Henley smiled. "You really needed that, didn't you?"

Darwin nodded.

"Are you done being upset with yourself?"

Darwin met Henley's gaze. "What do you mean?"

"You were so angry with yourself. Dean dying wasn't your fault, and I think you knew it deep down. But you didn't accept it. You couldn't fight the disease that took him, so you turned the anger you had on yourself. The only person you needed to finally forgive turned out to be you."

"You waited this long to tell me?"

Henley put their foreheads together. "I tried, Dare. So many times. But you weren't ready. You'd change the subject or walk away. Now I think I understand why. You needed to finally feel again, so you could purge the hurt."

A weight had lifted from Darwin's shoulders. The difference in his outlook surprised him. The hurt would never really go away completely. Dean had been too much a part of Darwin's life for that to happen. But now he truly felt ready to embrace life again. And Ricky was the one he wanted to embrace it with.

"Are you sure you have everything?" Henley asked for the dozenth time.

"Yes." Darwin took a breath, then started reciting the list of items he had tucked away. "I have my phone, a map in case the GPS unit in the car stops working, credit cards if I need to get gas or for when we stop for food. Pretty sure I'm all set."

Henley turned to Maria, who smiled at Darwin. "They grow up so fast, don't they?"

She laughed, but Darwin detected a note of pride in her expression. She'd been with the family for nearly forty years, and she loved him almost like a mother. After his parents died, she'd become the person he'd go to when he needed to talk. She'd make them each a cup of cocoa, and then sit there and listen as he poured out his heart.

She raised her hands and shooed them out of her kitchen. They turned and headed for the door.

"No, not you Darwin. Henley, you go find something to do," she snapped at the man. She loved him, though.

"Ooh, sounds like you're gonna get the talk about the birds and the bees."

Maria threw a croissant at him, and laughed when he caught it and stuffed it in his mouth. He went over and kissed her on the cheek, then hurried from the kitchen.

"Sit down," she ordered.

Darwin pulled a chair over to her counter and sat, watching as she chopped tomatoes for her homemade salsa.

"You seem different today," she mused.

"I feel different," he admitted.

"I'm glad. For too long you were so sad. I like this look on you much better."

With his cheeks flaming, Darwin leaned over and took a slice of tomato. "He's so different from Dean. He sees the world in a way I never have. Listening to him talk, watching as his eyes grow big when he tells me a story about something that excites him, or even the smile he shows when he's talking about the kitten he rescued." Darwin sighed, hoping this trip wouldn't end all that. "I think you'd like him, Maria."

"What do you mean you think I'd like him? You'll be bringing him to dinner soon. No, wait. If I say soon, you'll think I'm going to forget and put it off. Then I'm going to have to nag at you." She narrowed her eyes at him. "You'll ask him for dinner tomorrow night. No one gets close to my boy unless I get to meet them."

Darwin laughed, but the expression on her face clued him in to the fact she was dead serious.

"You can't... I mean..."

"Tomorrow, *niño*," she demanded, punctuating her insistence with a gentle finger poke to his chest. "I'll make him dinner, and you'll introduce us."

The idea had merit. Then a thought crossed his mind. "Could I invite his mother and sister, too?"

"No father?"

"No, he died."

"Oh, the poor boy." She clucked her tongue. "Yes, yes! Invite them all. It's been too long since I cooked for a family."

"You know, he doesn't really know me that well yet. He might not want to come."

"He'll come," she insisted. "Who couldn't love you?"

She turned away from her chopping and grabbed a pen and paper. She glanced over her shoulder and snapped, "What are you waiting for? Go and invite him."

She laughed, and that had Darwin laughing, too.

"What are you doing?" he asked, trying to peek over her shoulder.

"Making a shopping list. Find out what they like to eat, then let me know. I'll make a cheesecake for dessert. I'll go to the market and pick up some fresh berries, and make some homemade whipped cream." She gave him a glare. "Don't dilly dally! Get going. And, Darwin? Don't mess this up." She gave him a smile that never failed to warm his heart.

"Yes, ma'am." He saluted her and exited the kitchen. He wasn't surprised at all to find Henley waiting at the door.

"Invite him to dinner? Wow. She moves fast."

"And you're a snoop."

He shrugged and pushed off the wall. "Where do you think I learned all of the gossip we used to share when we were kids? Like that time the butler got the maid pregnant. Ooh, what a scandal that was."

"Well he *was* fifty-six at the time and married to the housekeeper. Mother and father certainly couldn't have that kind of impropriety going on under their roof."

"At least they didn't fire anyone. It really was nice of them to get them all jobs with separate families."

"That's only because it helped them save face. The scandal could have rocked a lot of lives."

Henley nodded in agreement.

Darwin rubbed his sweaty palms on his pants. "I should get going. I have to pick him up soon."

"Last chance. If you let me drive, the two of you can make out in the back of the car."

Darwin chuckled. "I think we'll be okay."

Henley wrapped him in a hug. "It's going to be fine, you know. Maria was right. Who couldn't love you?" He paused, then added, "Do you know how you're going to bring it up?"

"Yeah. I'd rather not say, though. It's an idea forming in my head, and if I say it out loud, it's going to sound stupid, and I'll stress about it."

Henley patted Darwin on the back, grinned, and said, "Then go get your man, tiger."

CHAPTER NINE

Ricky stepped outside his apartment and sucked in a breath of air. It had finally cooled off to the mid-seventies, thanks to a breeze off the lake. The sun shone high in the sky against a pale blue backdrop. He couldn't imagine a more beautiful day. He'd left the windows open, laughing as Merlin staked out a spot in the sun.

When Darwin pulled up, Ricky's eyes bugged out—a sleek white car with a Corvette logo, the hard top down, and Darwin with windblown hair and a sweet smile on his face. The man looked to be the epitome of cool.

"What kind of car is this?" he asked.

"Corvette Stingray. I wanted something special. Do you like it?"

Like? That word seemed too weak for Ricky's thoughts on the car. He'd always loved sporty cars. Their power thrilled him. When he'd been younger, his father would bring home magazines that showed muscle cars, sports cars, and concept cars. They'd sit on the couch and thumb through them, pointing out which ones they wanted. That would be how they'd spent every Saturday morning until his father died. But when he had the money, Ricky would still grab a magazine and relive the good times they'd shared.

"It's amazing. Is it yours?"

Darwin laughed. "No, I rented it for the day. I'm not sure I'd have a use for this car on a permanent basis. Are you ready to go?"

Ricky slid in, brushing his hand across the black leather seat. The interior gleamed, and the display showed all manner of features the car had available: Music, GPS, weather, phone. He couldn't believe how amazing it felt to be sitting in a machine like this.

"Buckle up," Darwin said. "We're ready to roll."

Ricky dutifully fastened his seatbelt and leaned back into the plush seat when the car jolted forward. He could feel the power, barely contained, that thrummed through his body. Darwin drove the speed limit, and the car seemed to be begging him to open up, let it show what it could do. Ricky was glad Darwin had driven, because he didn't think he'd be able to resist the car's entreaties.

The view along Lake Drive had always been one of Ricky's favorites. The blue water of Lake Michigan on one side, the spires of Chicago on the other. He felt as though he straddled a line between the two worlds. He closed his eyes and let the wind wash over him. And, of course, he drifted off.

When he woke, Darwin had parked the car outside a restaurant. It seemed to be tucked away in the corner of a bunch of buildings, mostly factories. He couldn't see how the place could stay in business, though. It didn't seem to belong here, one of those "if you didn't already know it was there, you'd miss it" places.

"Where are we?" he asked, stretching.

"Have a good nap?" Darwin teased, a knowing grin on his face.

"I'm sorry. I thought I'd be too keyed up to sleep."

"Don't apologize. You looked comfortable, so I figured I'd let you doze until we got here. The reviews on this place are incredible. It doesn't look like much from the outside, but their food is supposed to be amazing."

They got out of the car, and Darwin latched the roof. He directed Ricky inside, laughing when the bell above the door startled them both. Surprisingly, there were quite a few people already spread throughout the interior. They glanced up as Darwin and Ricky entered, one even gave a wave.

"Hi, boys. Take a seat anywhere. I'll be right with you," the waitress called.

They moved to the back and slid into one of the open booths. Ricky couldn't take his eyes off everything. It seemed like a throwback to the diners of the 1950s, with swivel seats at the long, curved counter. Tiled floors in geometric patterns. Even the outfit the server wore harkened back to an earlier time.

She handed them each a menu, and stood there while they looked it over. "Today's soup is vegetable. We've also got chili. It's kind of spicy, so you know. The special is chicken fried steak, served with mashed potatoes and gravy. If this is your first time here, you might want to try the Belly Buster. A sixteen-ounce sirloin burger, with six strips of bacon, cheddar and American cheese, served on a toasted bun. It comes with your choice of fries or onion rings."

"That's what I want," Darwin told her, putting his menu back on the table. "With the onion rings."

Ricky let his gaze drift over the menu. The smell of the food made his stomach rumble. He looked at the price of the burger, but then decided if Darwin would have it, so would he.

"Me, too, please. And could I have a strawberry shake?"

"They have shakes?" Darwin asked, grabbing his menu. "You didn't have them listed on the website."

"Which shows how often our site gets updated." She laughed. "We've had them for a good ten years now."

"I'd love a chocolate one, please. With a lot of whipped cream on top."

She smiled at them, then turned and headed for the kitchen.

They sat quietly for a few minutes, Ricky glancing around the restaurant. His mother would love this place. Then he caught himself and remembered they were on a date. Last thing anyone wanted would be to have their mother there. He coughed to cover a snicker, then turned his attention back to Darwin.

"That burger sounded amazing," Ricky admitted.

"I'm glad you didn't go for the salad."

"Yeah, I'm sure," Ricky said, allowing a little bit of attitude to creep in.

"Brat," Darwin retorted, then grinned.

"Takes one to know one," Ricky replied.

They kept up the banter for a few more minutes, though when the waitress returned, Ricky did his best to stifle the giggles.

"Are you guys like six? You sound like my boys," the waitress said, laughing as she put their shakes down.

"He acts like it," Ricky said, sticking out his tongue.

Darwin and their server, whose name tag said Emily, both laughed.

"Your food should be done pretty soon. Enjoy the shake."

"Thank you, Emily. I'm sure we will," Darwin replied, winking at her before she turned back toward the kitchen.

Ricky loved the shake. Thick, rich, and delicious. He glanced up at Darwin, and noticed his pinched expression. "You okay?"

Darwin put his glass down and took a deep breath. "We have to talk."

The way Darwin spoke put Ricky on alert. "That's never a good conversation starter," he mumbled.

"I've been trying to figure out a good time—a good way—to do this, but I just can't seem to think there will be one."

He reached into his pocket and pulled out a glossy sheet of paper.

"Please…look at this, and then you can ask me anything you want. I'm not doing it to freak you out or anything; you've got to believe that. But I can't keep on hiding things from you, because it isn't fair to either one of us."

He unfolded the sheet, then slid the paper across the table. Ricky saw Darwin's face smiling up at him. He looked resplendent in a charcoal tuxedo. "You're in a magazine article?"

Darwin nodded and his complexion seemed to take on a grayish tint.

Ricky turned his attention back to the page and read. The more he saw, the more twisted up his stomach became. He thought it might be a joke, but Financial News and Reports magazine really didn't seem to have much of a sense of humor.

"I...don't know what to say," Ricky stated, his stomach churning at the implications of what he'd seen. "So you're...what? CEO of a company?"

"Actually, I own it, too," Darwin replied quietly, looking down at the table.

"And it says you're on the NASDAQ," Ricky said, trying to process everything he'd seen. "So it's a good company?"

"I like to think so."

Ricky stood, the paper crumpled in his fist. "I need some air. I'll be back in a few minutes."

Darwin started to stand, but Ricky held out his hand.

"I need to be alone for a bit." He stumbled outside, his thoughts in a fog.

So Darwin had money. Big deal. Why should that matter? Only it did. Ricky had nothing, so what could he bring to a relationship? He sat down on the curb, pulled out his phone, and dialed.

"Two calls in less than two weeks? Wow, I must have done something right," his mother teased. "Wait. You'd tell me if I was dying, right? I mean you're not calling to see—"

Ricky's sob brought her up short.

"I'm sorry, honey. I didn't mean anything by it."

Ricky couldn't catch his breath. The pressure that squeezed his lungs made him feel as though he were drowning.

"Ricky? What's wrong? Talk to me. Do you need me to come and get you?"

"I-I-I... He... Mom?"

"Oh, baby. Please don't cry. Tell me what's bothering you. I can't help if you don't. Breathe."

He pulled in some air and blew it out slowly. Repeating the exercise several times helped to calm him a little.

"Do you want me to come get you?"

"No. It's not that. Mom, what would you have said if you found out Dad had a secret? One that made you feel as though you brought nothing to your relationship?"

"I don't think I understand."

Ricky unfurled the paper in his hand. "Darwin showed me a magazine article. He's the owner of Kincade International. He's rich, Mom. The magazine article says his net worth is close to six billion dollars. Why the hell would he want someone like me?"

"Because you're an amazing man?" she answered without hesitation. "Because he sees something in you that calls to him?" She paused. "Is he offering you money for sex?

"What? No!"

"Does he want to put you up in a fancy apartment so you'll be beholden to him?"

"Darwin's not like that, Mom."

"Then what are you really worried about?"

"He has money. More than anyone I know. I've got nothing. I can barely pay my bills and tuition."

"So you're not on equal footing with him. Would it make you feel better if he was poor? Do you care for the man or his pocketbook?"

"I don't care about his money," Ricky snapped.

"Then why are you letting it bother you? It's his money, sweetie. If he wants to do something with it, let him. Unless it makes you uncomfortable. Then you need to tell him. Do you understand? You said he's a good man. Then trust him. At least until he proves he can't be trusted. Then kick his ass."

Ricky snorted.

"Where are you now?"

"We drove down Lake Drive. I fell asleep, so I'm not really sure where we are. He took me to a small diner to get lunch."

"It sounds to me like he doesn't want you to be uncomfortable. Why not give him a chance to show you what kind of man he is?"

She was right. Darwin hadn't given Ricky any reason to doubt him. He could understand Darwin's fear at telling him the truth. After all, with how he'd reacted, he'd probably confirmed exactly how Darwin thought it would go.

"Thanks, Mom."

"I'm always there for you, Ricky. But if Darwin wants to buy me something, don't tell him no. Remind him I like sapphires. But only with platinum, because gold turns my skin green."

Ricky laughed. "I should go. I left him sitting in the restaurant."

"Go then. And just be true to who *you* are."

Ricky got up, brushed off his pants, and headed back to the restaurant. He glanced over at the car, and it brought a smile to his face. Darwin had done it to impress him. He didn't need to, though. Ricky had gone far beyond that stage already.

****

"He walked out," Darwin whimpered to his friend. He wanted to chase after Ricky, but to what end? If the man said he didn't want to see Darwin again, he wouldn't be able to stop him from walking away. "What the hell do I do now?"

"Breathe, Dare. Where did he go?"

"He told me he needed some air. Then he walked out the door."

"Then take him at his word. You just laid out a huge bit of news. It's no surprise that he's reeling."

Darwin twisted the napkin in his hand, tearing it into small pieces. "I should go after him. Maybe I can—"

"What? There's very little you can do. He'll either accept it or he won't. But it has to be on his terms. I know it sucks, and I'm real sorry for that. I wish I could make it all better."

The bell above the door rang, and Darwin twisted in his seat. When Ricky stepped in, Darwin breathed a sigh of relief and the knot in his stomach loosened a little. As soon as he slid into the booth, Darwin leaned forward. "I'm so sorry. I couldn't think of a better way to do it."

"It's fine," Ricky replied coolly.

"If you want, I can take you home."

A small smile played on Ricky's lips. "But we haven't eaten yet."

Darwin's head jerked up. "You mean you'll still eat with me?"

"Well, yeah. The burger sounded delicious." He reached out and touched Darwin's fingers. "And I really like the company."

"Darwin? Dare!"

"Oh, crap. One second." Darwin brought the phone back to his ear. "Sorry, he's back now."

"And are you over your panic?"

"For the moment. Thank you, Henley."

"Anytime. You know that."

They disconnected. Darwin pocketed his phone and turned his attention back to Ricky.

"Did you think I wouldn't come back?"

Darwin gave a half-shrug. "A little."

"So you called someone, too? I called my mom."

"I called Henley. He's my driver and best friend."

Ricky shook his head. "Your driver. Like a limo?"

"Yeah. Does it bother you?"

"Does it bother me? It freaks me the hell out. The magazine article said you were worth nearly six billion dollars."

Darwin grinned. "It's an old article."

He couldn't help but chuckle when Ricky started doing a fish impression.

"I really don't have all that money," Darwin explained. "We set up several charities across the US. We help to support shelters for runaway LGBT youth, battered women, and the like. Personally I give money to groups working on cures for cancers. I lost the first person I loved to the damned disease a few years ago, and I don't want anyone to go through that again."

"I'm sorry for your loss," Ricky said softly.

"Thank you. But I'm okay." They were quiet for a moment, then Darwin looked up as Emily brought their food. She couldn't have come at a better time. They both needed a little space to get their thoughts in order. Conversation could wait.

The burgers were delicious. Everything Emily said they would be. The best part? Watching Ricky turn his plate around, trying to figure out where to start on the monster burger.

"My eyes were bigger than my stomach," he said, then chuckled. "Belly Buster is a great name for this."

Though some residual tension remained in the air, and Darwin knew they had a lot to talk about, he found himself grateful that at least now he'd have the opportunity to do so.

****

"I'm glad you stuck around," Darwin said, turning the key in the ignition.

Ricky's fingers clenched. He had no idea what to say. He'd never talked to a man who had money. Now it seemed that whatever they would talk about, it most likely would be Darwin placating him. He didn't know about fancy things. To him, opera was either a browser or a bunch of people up on a stage shrieking.

"So what now?" he asked hesitantly.

"Sorry?"

Ricky glanced out at the countryside. He didn't think he could bear to look at Darwin, because he'd probably cry. "Well, I think we're both well aware that you're more traveled than me, more learned. I'm just a waiter. It's not like I can offer anything to you."

Darwin turned on his directional and pulled the car to the side of the road.

"Please tell me you're kidding."

Ricky fidgeted in his seat. "My mom told me you wanted to be with me because I'm supposed to be an amazing man. But compared to you…?"

Ricky left the rest of the sentence unspoken.

"Hey, come here." Darwin took Ricky's hand in his. "You listen to me, and you listen good. You want to know what you have to offer? I'll tell you. You brought me back to life. Almost literally.

112

When Dean, my late husband, passed, I felt so lost. I wandered through my days. My only joy happened to be at a restaurant you might be familiar with. A waiter I liked to ogle worked there, but then one day he left. I acted out a little to the new server that came to me."

Ricky tried to work up a smile at the compliment, but he couldn't manage it. He glanced over at Darwin, who sat there looking at him like Ricky was something precious. Thoughts of what he could say deserted him, though.

"You'd like him" Darwin continued. "He had a smile that lit up the room. He didn't take any crap from me. When I acted like a jerk, he called me on it. But when I said I should go? He worried enough that he wanted me to eat. And then, this guy did the most astounding thing. Instead of selling me a line about the food they served there? He told me about his favorite food. I'd never had a corn dog before. And as I sat there eating it, I realized there were so many things I'd never had.

"So I started wondering. What else could this man teach me about life? So far he's taught me the joy of dancing, even if I did it badly. The tickle in my throat from a delicious local ale. How amazing it is to sit across from someone and share a meal. How much I missed being hugged, kissed…hell, just being touched."

Ricky could hear the emotion creeping into Darwin's voice. It broke as he spoke, and Ricky wanted to hug him close, but those niggling thoughts about the differences between them stilled his hand.

"He taught me the joy of small things, like buying something for his cat. He made me laugh at the image of said cat lounging on the air conditioner unit. He made me feel…normal, at least for a while."

"Yes, but you could have done all those things without me. It's not like you don't have the money for them."

"Oh, Ricky," Darwin said softly. "The old adage is truer than you know. Money really can't buy happiness. All the stuff in the world that money can buy won't fill the hole inside of you."

Ricky choked back a laugh. His emotions were all over the place. Needing to get the conversation back to somewhere neutral, he said, "And here I thought my big news would be the most exciting part of the day."

"You have news? Tell!"

"Well, it's kind of insignificant next to yours. I got the job at Rossi's. I start Monday."

Darwin reached over and cupped Ricky's chin. He tried to pull him closer, but the seatbelt held him in place.

"Damn it," he snarled. "When we stop, remind me I owe you a hug and a kiss. Congratulations! I'm so happy for you."

Darwin seemed genuinely thrilled for Ricky. And that went a long way to soothing his jangled nerves.

They drove on, heading back toward home and real life. As they neared Ricky's building, Darwin blew out a breath and said, "Maria, my cook, wants me to invite your family over for dinner tomorrow night. She'd like to meet you, if that's okay."

"Dinner at your house? Tomorrow? With my family? You haven't met my mother," Ricky stated with a laugh.

"No, but I'd like to," Darwin replied, his tone showing his sincerity. "If she's anything like her son, I'm sure I'll…really like her."

Ricky sucked in a breath. "Isn't that a little fast?"

"Yes. It's completely and totally crazy," Darwin acknowledged. "But it feels right, at least to me. I can't explain it. If you're not ready, I very much understand, but I'd really like to meet your family and have you meet mine."

Ricky groaned. His mother would probably take the opportunity to embarrass him. The fact that Darwin wanted to meet his family warmed his heart, though. Of course, his family would probably be a lot more low class than the people Darwin knew. Ricky fretted that it might not be such a good idea after all.

CHAPTER TEN

"You're sure about this?" Ricky's mom asked for the millionth time since they'd gone outside to wait for Darwin.

"He said he wanted to meet you. I tried to warn him, but he still insisted."

She flicked his ear, which caused him to dance away, laughing.

"What time is he supposed to pick—"

"I told you, Mom, he'll be here in a few minutes. God, you're so damned impatient."

She glared at him, but her smile showed him she wasn't annoyed at all.

"You start your new job tomorrow, right?"

"I do," he replied.

"I'm going to get some of my friends and we're going to come down there and sit at one of your tables."

Ricky shuddered. He knew she would. "Sorry, Mom."

His mother cackled, which made Ricky and his sister laugh along with her.

When Ricky noticed the long, sleek limousine turn the corner, his mouth went dry. Darwin had said he'd pick them up, but he hadn't expected him to come in his limo. He glanced around, hoping no one saw the ostentatious display. Having his neighbors see this, and then start teasing him? Totally the last thing he needed.

The car stopped and a good-looking man stepped out of the driver's seat. Dark hair, with just a touch of premature gray peeking out from under the smart cap he wore. Slate gray eyes made him look cold and calculating, but Darwin had told him that although Henley looked tough, he was a true pussycat. Usually.

The man stepped around the car and pulled open the back door. Darwin sat there, looking every bit like the man holding court. Ricky swallowed.

"Good evening. I'd get out to introduce myself, but Maria said if I didn't have you back to the house promptly by seven, not to bother coming home at all."

Ricky's mother and sister laughed, then slid into the car. Henley tipped his hat to them as they entered. Ricky got in last, taking the seat beside Darwin. Henley closed the door, then went back to the driver's side and got in.

The smell of leather enhanced Darwin's natural aroma and warmth, making it hard for Ricky to breathe without devilish thoughts popping into his head. He discreetly placed his hands across his lap. When he looked up, his sister waggled her brows at him, and Ricky stifled a groan. Leave it to Trish to notice his discomfort.

"Since my son is too rude to introduce us, this is my daughter Trish. I'm Megan Donnelly."

"It's a pleasure to meet you both. Ricky's talked fondly about you."

Ricky's mom snorted. "You don't have to try to cover his shortcomings. Not like I don't already know about them."

"Mom," Ricky whined.

She laughed and turned her attention back to Darwin. "I love your car."

A slight pink creeped up Darwin's neck. "Thank you. We would have brought the regular one, but Henley thought we should make a show of it."

"Plus the fact that I picked it out," Henley called from the front seat.

"He did," Darwin admitted. "I like the small and sporty one. He wanted ridiculously long so you'd see it. Personally, I think he's a size queen. We compromised and got both. I don't usually use this one, though. As for the man driving, that's Henley. My full time driver and sometimes best friend."

"Ooh, your razor wit draws blood, Dare," Henley responded, not taking his eyes off the road.

The rest of the trip to Darwin's house had Trish and Ricky's mom peppering him with questions. They ran the gamut from how did the two of them meet to what kind of work Kincade International did. Darwin answered them all with great aplomb.

When Henley informed them that they'd arrived, Ricky looked up, and the air whooshed from his lungs as if he'd been punched. Darwin kept saying house, but the place that lay before them wasn't a house. It was a freaking mansion. The trip up the circular drive took nearly five minutes, during which time Ricky noted the immaculately sculpted topiaries, the dark green grass trimmed uniformly, and the giant marble fountain that stood dead center amongst it all, with fish spraying water into a basin lit with all the colors of the rainbow.

Henley opened the door, held out a hand for the ladies, and stood back as Ricky stepped out. He'd never seen a place like this before, and his discomfort continued to rise as they walked toward the door.

From what little he could see of the outside, the place took up a lot of space. Ricky couldn't even see the full building. It stood three stories tall, with enormous windows that had to be a pain to clean. At first glance, the exterior seemed to be made of stone, but as Ricky stepped up onto the open-air porch, he could see the hewn wood with a cream-colored paint that had been done in such a way as to resemble sandstone blocks.

"The estate is called Kincade Manor. Built around 1820 by Augustus Kincade as a gift to his young wife Alicia, it was the preeminent destination for those who wanted to be seen. When Augustus died at eighty, his sons inherited it. One of the boys, Emil, had already built a successful life as a lawyer in Wisconsin and had no desire to come back to Illinois, so he gifted his part of the bequest to his brother, Thaddeus. Rumor had it that old Thad was gay and never had children. When he died, he left it to his nephew, Jeremiah. After that things get a bit hazy what with the Civil War. The house changed hands more than once, falling from the family due to misfortune of the times. About sixty years ago, my grandfather bought it back and had it restored to what it is today."

Trish and Ricky's mom stood in awe as Darwin opened the front doors of the mansion. The sick, twisted feeling that had settled in Ricky's gut exploded throughout his body at the sight of crystal chandeliers refracting the light into luminous cascades of color that danced around the ornate entryway.

They were met by an older gentleman, maybe sixty. He asked for and took their coats, then hung them up in a closet that seemed enormous. While Ricky stared, the man cleared his throat, drawing Ricky's attention. They were led through the house as Darwin pointed out some of the features, like being the first house in the area with actual plumbing and electricity.

Ricky barely heard what Darwin said. He couldn't take his eyes off the place. His whole apartment would fit in the damned entryway. Snakes slithered through his gut as the enormity of the differences between him and Darwin hit home. With every word that Darwin spoke, the chasm between the two of them seemed to become more impossible to bridge.

When the man—butler?—finally opened the door to the dining room, everything Ricky thought of as being rich went out the window. The table appeared to be carved from an enormous single piece of wood, then highly polished. You could see the knots and grain clearly through whatever coated it. He did a quick count, and winced as he found space for eighteen people around the table. Who the hell even knew that many people?

Darwin thanked the man who'd guided them in. He gave a half-bow and exited through the door they'd used to come in.

"Okay, we're about to enter the inner sanctum. Maria is looking forward to meeting you, and we'll start with the first course in about fifteen minutes. She's got canapés in the kitchen if anyone is feeling a little hungry."

When Darwin ushered them into the kitchen, the gleam of copper cookware hanging over the kitchen island caught Ricky's attention. Of everything he'd seen so far, the kitchen appeared to be the warmest and most inviting room. It seemed out of place in the palatial home, looking as though it would fit perfectly in a rustic bed and breakfast. The cabinets were rough-hewn wood with leaded glass windows. Marble countertops were filled with odds and ends, and a harried-looking woman stood on the other side of them, her hands a blur as she measured and chopped.

"This gem of a woman is Maria. She's been part of the family for a while now—in other words, she said if I told you how old she was, she'd refuse to feed me—and we love having her here."

Darwin reached across the counter and picked up a piece of tomato, which earned him a thwack on the hand from the wooden spoon Maria snatched up.

"If you want food, go grab the trays and hand them out. Or get the so-called *waiters* in here. Those lazy asses haven't done anything all day to help their mama."

Ricky's mom snickered, and that earned her a bright smile from Maria.

"How do you do? I'm Maria Gonzales." She held out a hand, then drew it back. "My apologies. I forgot I'm not really presentable right now."

Darwin leaned over and kissed her on the cheek. "You're gorgeous, and I don't ever want to hear you say otherwise. And be nice to your boys. They're good kids. They take after their mother."

Her skin darkened slightly, and she gazed up at Darwin, blatant affection in her eyes.

"Did you want to eat here or in the formal room? I need to have those useless boys set the table."

Darwin pulled Ricky to the side. "It's up to you. Do you want the whole experience, or would you rather it be more intimate? We have two waiters standing by, so we can do either."

Ricky couldn't believe what Darwin asked. The thought of eating in that massive room had his stomach doing flips. He'd never felt so out of place anywhere before. "In here, please," he whispered.

"We'll eat in here, Maria."

"Tomás! You and your brother get out here and get ready for our guests."

Two young teens stepped into the kitchen. They were dressed in burgundy vests with crisp white shirts and black pants with razor sharp pleats, and except for their ages, they'd look at home in any high-class restaurant.

"Good evening, Mister Darwin. How many will be dining this evening?"

"Four of us, please Martín. We'll be eating in this room, so once the meal is served, we won't be needing your service."

"Oh, no!" Maria shouted. "When they put down dinner, there are plenty of pots that need washing, and a floor that could use a good scrubbing."

"Maria?" Darwin said, his brow furrowing.

She huffed. "Fine. They can do them tomorrow."

Darwin smiled. "Thank you."

The two servers picked up the trays and started passing finger food around. It all seemed so silly to Ricky. It wasn't as if they couldn't help themselves. When one of them, Tomás, Ricky thought, held out the silver platter to him, Ricky shook his head. The young waiter gave him a big smile before he moved on to the next person.

"Dinner will be ready in a minute," Maria called out.

"Time to sit." Darwin pulled out the chairs for Ricky's mother and sister, then took his place at the head of the table. Ricky watched as one of the brothers collected a tureen from their mother, then carefully ladled soup into the waiting bowls, while the other put down baskets of piping hot rolls.

"This is Mexican beef soup," Tomás said. "It's our grandmother's recipe that mama has adapted. She left out the meat in case anyone is vegetarian," he explained.

"I wouldn't have had to if *someone* had done what I asked so I knew what to make."

"I said I was sorry," Darwin said petulantly. "It wasn't like you gave me a lot of time to get this together."

Ricky glanced over at Maria, who had a slight grin on her face. She seemed perfectly at ease in her kitchen. His first bite of the soup had him wanting to beg for the recipe. He could taste the spices and herbs, the lime juice, and the garlic. Chunks of potato and cabbage swirled in the rich dark broth. Despite the uncomfortable weight in his stomach, Ricky grabbed a roll and slathered it with butter.

"This is so good," he moaned, then shifted his gaze down to his plate.

Maria stepped up behind him and lightly pinched his cheek. "This is a good boy, Darwin. He knows how to make an old woman feel proud."

"He's a suck-up," Ricky's mother said. "He never compliments my food."

"Maybe that's because your food isn't this good, Mom," Trish teased.

"You raise them, and they turn into such asses," his mother snapped.

Ricky's cheeks heated in embarrassment at his mother's language, but Maria laughed and said she couldn't agree more.

After their bowls were emptied, Maria's sons cleared them away, then put down a small salad with thick chunks of what appeared to be mango and avocado.

"This salad is a little sweet and just a bit spicy. It has mango, avocado, red cabbage, and mama's homemade cilantro-lime dressing. Just between us, it's probably the only salad I like."

And Ricky enjoyed it, too. Sweet and tart commingled with just the right amount of heat to give Ricky's tongue a slight burn.

"Make sure you save room, though. Mama has made something special for dinner, and she's nervous about how it will turn out."

"Martín!" Maria let fly with a string of words that Ricky didn't understand. Darwin's cheeks turned a bright red, and the two boys giggled and hurried out of the kitchen.

"She's telling them what ungrateful kids they are, then threatening to take away their video games," Darwin said, his cheeks almost scarlet.

"I speak a little Spanish, and that definitely wasn't their video games she was threatening," Trish said.

"I am so sorry," Maria apologized. "They're good boys, even if sometimes they need to be disciplined. Unfortunately, Darwin refuses to do it."

"Please," Darwin said, frowning at Maria. "Your kids are way more afraid of you than of me. Hell, *I'm* afraid of you."

That comment set everyone but Ricky to laughing. He wasn't sure why. It had been funny. But he couldn't get it out of his head that his family had come to a mansion for dinner with a man who had his staff serving them. The worst part about it? His mother and sister seemed to be perfectly at ease.

After the boys came back and cleared away the plates, they put down the main course. It smelled absolutely delicious and reminded Ricky of the cannelloni they served at Rossi's.

"This is a recipe I got from the internet—"

"That we had to help her find," Martín said with a laugh.

"It has pan-roasted wild mushrooms, shallots, thyme, and a blend of other mushrooms. The sauce is made with sweet potatoes, so if anyone doesn't like it, I have other things I can cook for you."

"Are you kidding?" Trish declared. "This smells amazing."

"Thank you for your kind words," Maria said, preening just a little.

Ricky pushed his plate away. Trish wasn't wrong, the food did smell great, but his stomach clenched, to an almost painful level. He stood and glanced around the table.

"I think I need to go home," he said. "I'm not feeling so well."

His mom stood and put her hand on his forehead, just as she'd done when he was little. "You're kind of clammy. What's wrong?"

He wanted to say his stomach, but Maria cast nervous glances at him, and he had no desire to upset her.

"I've got a headache," he lied. "Maybe a migraine coming on."

His mother gave him one of her patented looks that told him she knew better, because Ricky had never suffered a migraine before. "Why don't you go lie down on the sofa. Would that be okay, Darwin?"

"You can rest in the guest room if you'd like," came the reply.

"No, I left my pills at home. I think I should probably just go. Thank you for dinner, Maria. You're amazing."

His eyes burned as the force of his discomfort hit him. He needed to be out of here. Away from this place where he didn't belong. Where he would never belong.

"I can have Henley take you home," Darwin said softly.

Ricky could see the sadness in Darwin's expression. He'd put that there, and he had no idea how to take it away.

"No, that's okay. I'll make it home. Besides, you have guests."

"At least let me call you a cab, okay?" Darwin asked, slipping an arm around Ricky's waist.

Ricky nodded. His lungs started to ache, and he couldn't seem to draw in a decent breath.

"You all go ahead and eat," Darwin said. "I'm going to walk Ricky out. After dinner, we'll have dessert, and then we can take you home."

Ricky's mom started to follow, but he held up his hand. "Eat, Mom. Enjoy. I'll call you tomorrow."

After he retrieved his jacket, the stepped out onto the veranda, when Darwin turned to Ricky.

"I'm sorry. I know it's a lot to take in. I really wanted to impress your family. Seems I botched that."

He put his hands on the railing.

"It's not that," Ricky argued. "I just—I don't know how I should feel."

Darwin nodded. "I get it. Really. I've been wrestling with that myself. This is so different for me, but not for the same reasons. I like you, Ricky. A lot. You've opened my eyes to so many things I didn't realize I was missing out on. But you're uncomfortable, and I think you might need some time to think about it.

"I know you're starting the new job tomorrow, so how about if we just do some phone calls. Get back to a comfort zone. Then we'll see where we're at."

"Okay," Ricky said softly. He couldn't believe he could walk away from Darwin. He'd halfway fallen for the man the first night in the restaurant, but when he'd brought the corn dogs in for dinner? That had pushed him over into the love column quickly.

Darwin called for the cab, and the two of them sat on an old wooden swing at the end of the porch. The night should have been comfortable, but a chill coursed through Ricky, and the depth of it scared him.

When the cab pulled up, Darwin walked him down to the drive. He paid the driver, despite Ricky's protest, then hugged him. As soon as the warmth enveloped him, the tears started streaming down his face.

"Good night, Ricky," Darwin whispered, then hurried back into the house.

"Good-bye, Darwin," Ricky replied.

CHAPTER ELEVEN

The next two weeks they spoke sporadically. With Ricky training, Darwin didn't want to interrupt him, no matter how much he missed hearing that voice. The times they did talk, the conversation stayed purposely light. Neither of them brought up the magazine article or the awkward dinner, and Darwin felt at peace with that.

Henley, however, wasn't pleased at all. He picked Darwin up after work Friday evening, as per usual. Darwin sat in the back and pulled from his briefcase some files Kent had passed along. Darwin studied Kent's proposal and had to admit his brother's whole plan was truly ingenious. The company that owned the product marketed it as a garbage disposal, but Kent's team had turned it into a composting waste recycle center. With a few technically minor modifications, Kent could create something that would help rid cities of millions of tons of garbage each year, turning it into rich topsoil.

"We're here," Henley snapped.

Darwin looked up. They weren't home. Instead they were parked outside of Rossi's.

"What's going on, Henley?"

"Tonight the two of you are going to talk," Henley said, his tone harsh. "I don't know about you, but I'm sick of the fact that you go into work early and stay later than anyone except the cleaners. I get that you don't want to bother Ricky while he's learning a new job. That's commendable. But avoiding the situation won't make it any better. And to be honest, you're kind of turning into a dick."

"Excuse me?"

"What did Maria make you for breakfast this morning?"

Darwin tried to recall. She always made him something special, but he couldn't come up with what it had been.

"Scrambled eggs with chorizo. Your favorite. She didn't like seeing you mope around the house like a puppy that someone kicked. She thought maybe it would perk you up. You didn't even say thank you. I told her I'd talk to you, but she insisted it was fine."

It wasn't. Not one bit. Maria would be one of the last people Darwin would ever want to hurt. She took such good care of him and the few people who remained on staff.

"I'll apologize."

"Oh, hell no. You apologize to her, and I'm going to end up with my privates on her cutting board. That woman is ruthless. What you will do is go see Ricky. Talk to the man. Get whatever is bugging the two of you out in the open and deal with it. Enough of this pussyfooting around."

Darwin hated when Henley was right.

"But I don't have a reservation," he wheedled.

"I had Heather make one at eight o'clock in Ricky's station."

A low growl rumbled from Darwin. "You know, I can fire you."

"Then do it," Henley snapped. He raised his chin defiantly. "Right now, I think I'd rather look for a new job than watch you self-destruct anymore."

The venom in Henley's words rattled Darwin. He'd never heard so much barely restrained anger from the man. He figured he should listen. Finally.

****

Ricky couldn't believe how busy the night had been. He'd had two parties of eight, and a couple of four-tops that had kept him jumping. Fortunately, Bertie staggered the parties, so even though he'd run his butt off, it hadn't been overwhelming.

He'd loved every minute of it. The fact that they already trusted him with parties like this meant a lot. And the customers? Oh, damn.

While the tips weren't quite as good as they'd been at Asiago, the guests he had weren't tense or snooty. The families that had come with their kids seemed to adore him, as he took great care in making sure the children felt like they were part of the evening. Several commented on how well behaved their kids were when he included them.

He glanced up at the clock. Almost eight. He had one booth in his station that had a reserved sign on it. Unless it got busy again, this would be his last table of the evening. He finished clearing the dishes from the seventieth birthday party of Bertie's mother—and what a hoot she'd been—and poured a couple glasses of water for his next guests.

When he heard Bertie approaching with his people, and that smooth as velvet voice he knew so well washed over him, Ricky hesitated. It couldn't be. He hadn't seen Darwin in two weeks and, if he were honest, he really didn't think he could handle seeing him now.

He'd gone online and done some research on the man. He found out how he lost his first love and read the articles about how it seemed to impact him and his business. But the more he discovered, the less comfortable he felt. Darwin knew the governor, for fuck sake. As if that hadn't been bad enough, he discovered a picture of him with the goddamn president. He'd shut the computer off after that and hadn't even bothered to look any deeper.

When he turned around, he tried to put a smile on his face, but he knew it would look false. No way could he pretend around Darwin. The man deserved better.

"Good evening. Welcome to Rossi's. My name is Ricky. Would you like to start with an appetizer this evening? Perhaps something from the bar? We've got a very nice glass of Kendall-Jackson merlot that would pair well with several of the specials for tonight."

When he looked up and met Darwin's gaze, a pain seared through Ricky's heart. The man looked demolished. His eyes had

Prada-size bags beneath them. It took all Ricky could manage not to slide into the booth and pull Darwin close.

"Hi, Ricky."

The voice still gave him goose bumps, but it sounded weary. Sad, even.

"Hey, Darwin. Look, I really can't—"

"I know. Henley kidnapped me and dragged me down here. How've you been?"

"Oh, fine." The light tone he'd tried for was proved a lie when his voice cracked. He'd been anything but okay. He missed Darwin. More than he ever thought he could miss anyone. But, now that he had come in, Ricky knew the time to lay out what he'd been thinking had arrived.

"Listen, Darwin. I've been thinking. I'm not sure it's a good idea for the two of us to see one another. We're from two different worlds, and I know that I can't fit into yours. I'll never be the sleek, polished guy you need on your arm at events, and I doubt you'd be happy going to auto shows with me."

Darwin looked stricken, and a low throb started building in Ricky's chest.

"I had a great time with you, but I think we should maybe call it quits."

Darwin didn't speak. He nodded, then slid out of the booth and rushed for the door. Ricky wanted to call after him, tell him he'd been wrong, beg him to stay, but what good would it do? No matter what, they'd never be compatible.

As soon as the door closed behind him, Bertie came up. "He decided not to eat?"

"Yeah. He had a meeting or something he got called to."

"Okay. Then since it's slow, you can go if you want."

Ricky nodded mutely. "Thanks. I think I will.

He headed back to the lockers to change, so he could go home to his empty apartment. Hopefully Merlin would be in a talking mood tonight, because Ricky really didn't feel like being alone.

****

"I hope you're fucking happy!" Darwin snapped as he approached the limousine. "Every goddamn one of you."

"Calm down, Dare. What happened?"

"He dumped me. Told me we weren't meant to be together." Darwin's voice continued to rise, and they got looks from people leaving the restaurant, but he didn't care.

"Did he say why?"

"Apparently we're too different. My having money makes me unsuitable to date him. To…love him."

"Aw, Dare. I'm sorry." He put a hand on Darwin's shoulder. "Let's go home."

"No," Darwin shouted, twisting away as if the touch burned.

"Okay, where do you want to go?" Henley asked, as if trying to soothe a child.

"With you? Nowhere. I would have been happy with what we had. Talking to him on the phone would be better than not talking to him at all. But now I don't even get that." His hands clenched, and it took everything in Darwin to not lash out. "I'm going back to the office."

"Okay, I'll drive—"

"No. I don't want to see you—anyone—tonight. I'll stay there. Tell Maria not to make breakfast for me."

With that, he turned and stormed down the street. Even though it would be a long walk, Darwin didn't care. He didn't want anyone trying to talk to him. To tell him that maybe Ricky had been right.

But he wasn't, Darwin was sure of it. They'd been good together. Had fun. It had meant something to both of them. Maybe he could salvage this. It shouldn't be that hard. He pulled out his phone, found the number he needed, and dialed.

"Hey, Darwin."

"Kent? I need to see you and Mila in my office, please."

"Is something wrong? It's almost eight-thirty."

"I know it's late, but if you can manage it, I'd really appreciate seeing the two of you." He'd put an end to this tonight, one way or another.

He heard Kent talking to Mila in the background, then he came back and said, "Sure, can you give us an hour?"

Darwin chuckled. "That would be great. It'll take me that long to get back."

"Is everything okay?" The tone of concern in Kent's voice warmed Darwin. It had been so long since he'd heard it.

"I think it will be."

He disconnected the call, then started walking again. He half-expected Henley to pull up behind him, but when that didn't happen, Darwin breathed a sigh of relief. He'd never been so angry with his friend. It wasn't anyone's fault but his, though. Still, at least with the plan he had in mind, there might be a way to put things to right.

His feet ached by the time he made it to Kincade International. The shoes he wore looked great, but weren't meant to be used to walk two miles over rough roads. When he arrived, Mitch from Security let him in.

"You're here awful late, Mr. Kincade. Everything okay?"

"Yes, I've got some work to do. My brother and his wife will be arriving soon."

"They're already here, sir. I sent them on up to your office."

"Thank you. I appreciate it."

He got on the private elevator that delivered him to his suite. Mila sat in one chair, while Kent occupied the other. As Darwin walked in, Kent stood and covered the distance between them in four long strides.

"What's going on? I have to admit, you're kind of scaring us."

Darwin waved at the chair. "Sit, please. This shouldn't take long."

Kent went back to Mila, sat down, and clutched her hand, his expression grim.

"I'm not going to beat about the bush. I want you and Mila to step up and take over Kincade, just like you should have done from the beginning."

The eerie silence disturbed Darwin.

"Kent? Is something wrong?"

"No, I understand the question. I just don't understand why."

A myriad of excuses floated through Darwin's head. But the only one that seemed acceptable pushed out of his mouth. "I'm tired. I need to do something for me. I can't do this job anymore, because the cost is just too high."

"What happened?" Mila asked.

He didn't want to tell them. It shouldn't matter. But they sat there, looking at him expectantly. He sighed. "I fell in love."

"That doesn't preclude you from running the company. We handle it."

"Yes, the two of you. Together. The person I love sees my money as a blockade between the two of us. I can't let that happen."

Mila stood and rushed to Darwin, pulling him to her.

"Honey, you're always going to have money. Even if we took over the company, you still have your inheritance, stocks, bonds. You can't get rid of it all."

"I can donate it," Darwin insisted. "Give it to charities that can make good use of it."

"To what end, Dee? Are you sure this will make...Ricky, right?"

Darwin nodded.

"Will this make Ricky happy? How do you think he'll feel knowing you gave up your life for him?"

Logically Kent made sense, but Darwin wasn't interested in making sense. He wanted to be with Ricky, no matter what it took.

"If you do this, and he still rejects you, what will you do?"

"I don't know," Darwin wailed. "But I can't do nothing. I love him."

"I believe you do, but how does he feel? Are you sure it's the money, or is that an excuse? You can't change who you are for someone."

"Why?" Darwin yelled. "You did."

"No, I did it for me. I didn't like who I was and realized that I needed a change. Mila helped with that. Huge difference."

"Why won't you just help me? I gave you money for your company. I didn't ask for anything in return. Please. Just do this for me."

Kent glanced over at his wife, and she nodded.

"Okay, fine. We'll do it. But you have to know, it's under protest. We think you're making the worst decision possible."

Darwin slumped in his chair, relief coursing through him. He'd see it got done. He'd call his lawyers tonight; tell them to prepare the paperwork. He wanted this done swiftly, no matter what it cost. He'd gladly change his whole life if it brought Ricky back to him.

****

Ricky sat on the chair, rubbing Merlin between the ears. He'd long ago put his phone on speaker and placed it on the table next to him. It was almost midnight, and his mother had been berating him for nearly an hour. That came after Trish talked his ear off for almost two.

"You're being stupid," she insisted.

"No, I'm not! He's had dinner with a president, Mom. A fucking president. I can see it now. Me all dressed up in a tux, walking into that dining room which will be filled with beautiful people, and the president comes over, shakes my hand, and asks who I am. I'll tell him I'm Ricky Donnelly. He'll ask what I do, and I'll smile ever so sweetly and say, 'I wait tables at a restaurant.'"

"So? I don't understand. Being a server is an honest profession. A good one. Why should you be ashamed of it?"

Ricky took a deep breath. They were going around in circles and getting absolutely nowhere.

"I'm not, Mom. I like being a server. But it's not something you say to the president of our country. Hell, even if I open my own place, it's still nowhere near important enough to brag about."

She sighed. "I don't know what to say. The man is crazy about you, and you're just going to dump him because you feel bad. Your father taught at the college. I was a homemaker with two kids. Do you think your father thought of me as less than him? Do you think I saw myself as being not as good because he had a better education and job?"

"It's different, Mom. You know it is," Ricky protested.

"No, honestly, I really don't." She sighed. "I'm tired. I'll talk to you tomorrow, honey."

She hung up, and Ricky felt the weight of his decision crashing down on him. He'd made the best choice he could. Why couldn't anyone understand it? Darwin needed someone from his own world, more like himself. Someone who could make him look good. Ricky definitely wasn't that person.

When his door buzzer rang, Ricky thought it might be Darwin. Part of him hoped it was, but the larger part prayed it wouldn't be. He decided he'd ignore whoever it was, because he didn't think he could face Darwin right now.

A few minutes later, a knock at the door startled Ricky. He got up and turned the knob. When the door swung open, the very last person he expected to see stood before him.

"Hey, Ricky. We need to talk."

Chapter Twelve

Ricky couldn't believe it when he opened the door to find Darwin's driver standing there. He peeked around the corner, expecting to see the man himself, but Henley shook his head. "I'm alone," he assured Ricky.

"How did you get up here? I didn't buzz you in."

"There was this little old lady coming in carrying a bunch of groceries. I offered to help, and she got me in."

"That would be Mrs. Metzger."

"Yeah, that's her," Henley said, a big smile gracing his face. "She's a sweetheart. I'm invited back next week for hot and sour cabbage soup." Henley rubbed his stomach. "I can't wait."

Ricky chuckled. "Her son doesn't visit enough, but when he comes, she makes all kinds of cabbage things for him." Ricky paused. "Is Darwin with you?"

"It's just me. I was hoping we could talk."

"About what?" Ricky asked suspiciously.

Henley frowned. "Please. You already know about what."

"Did Darwin ask you to come?"

"Oh, God no. He'd be pissed if he knew."

The words put Ricky at ease. He stepped back and let Henley into the apartment.

"This is…nice."

"It's awful. You don't need to be diplomatic. Right now it's all I can afford."

Ricky could see Henley wanted to say something, but he cut him off before he could.

"Can I get you something to drink? I have…well, water. I could probably make some coffee, too. Not sure if I have enough for a full pot, though."

"No, I'm fine. I just came to talk. Can we sit?"

Ricky shooed Merlin off the chair, then waved his hand. "Go ahead."

Henley took the chair and immediately found himself with a lapful of cat. Merlin rubbed against him, before snuggling down on his lap.

"Cats usually hate me," Henley said, rubbing Merlin's ears.

"Merlin thinks he's a dog," Ricky replied. "He's affectionate, likes to cuddle, and will run and grab things I throw then bring them back."

"He seems like a sweetheart."

Ricky sat across from Henley. "So, not to be rude or anything, but what's going on?"

Henley glanced up, then dipped his head and went back to stroking the cat.

"Why did you break up with Dare?" he asked cautiously.

Ricky's cheeks heated. "Excuse me?"

"I know it's not any of my business—"

"You're right," Ricky snapped. "If Darwin wanted to know, he could have come and talked to me himself."

He could see the flush on Henley's neck as the man stood, dislodging Merlin from his seat, which earned him a hiss that Henley ignored. "Because you would have let him in? I highly doubt that. You're so goddamn scared to talk to him you would have slammed the door in his face. So don't sit there and try to be indignant, because we both know it's a load of shit."

Ricky stared at Henley. The man had seemed so mild-mannered, and to hear him speak like that could only be called shocking. But he wasn't about to let anyone use that tone with him.

"Fuck you," he growled, jumping up and pointing a finger at Henley. "The man lied to me. He pretended to be something he wasn't. Then when he tells me who he is, he invites me to his house for dinner and shows up in his limousine. I find out that he lives in a mansion, has servants, and everything I think I know about him turns out to be, as you say, a load of shit."

Henley took a deep breath. "See? Right there. That shows that you don't know Dare at all. You didn't even give him a chance. That mansion, as you call it, has most of the wings closed off. Darwin didn't want the place, but he also didn't want to give up his family home. He tried to get his brother to take it, but he's not interested. The staff? There's seven of us, if you include Maria's kids. A cook who feeds us, a butler who spends his days pottering around in the garden, a driver whose only duty is to take Darwin to and from work. The rest of the time he drives Maria to the store so she can do the shopping. There's also a laundress who's probably seventy, and she only takes care of two rooms. She washes the clothes, but Darwin folds his own, and every morning, he makes his bed. We have a household manager who pays the bills and our wages. Everyone but the manager lives on the estate.

Henley dropped back onto the chair, Merlin assuming his original spot. "Those of us who work there do so because we love Darwin. All of them worked for his parents, helped to raise him to be the man he is. When they died, we stayed with him. When he inherited the estate, he tried to cut back, because he didn't want to be *that* guy. The showy, flashy guy. But the thing of it is? He never was.

"When his first love died, he shut himself off. He closed off almost all of the rooms, helped the staff find new jobs, but we few who still work there wouldn't leave him. Eventually we got him to listen to reason, but he wouldn't hire anyone else.

"So don't think you know the man, because all you're seeing is the money."

Ricky cocked his head. He could hear the truth in Henley's voice, but something else lay beneath the surface. "You're in love with him."

Henley averted his gaze. "That's ridiculous. He's my best friend."

136

"Who you happen to be in love with. Trust me, I've read enough romance novels. I know the signs." Ricky leaned against the table. "Have you told him?"

Henley opened his mouth, sure to protest, then closed it. He shook his head. "He doesn't feel that way about me. He was my first kiss, and I had it bad for him for years after. When he met Dean, I admit I got jealous. But the two of them fit, and Darwin…you could see how much love there was between them. I knew nothing would ever come of it. I moved on, but there's always that little part of me that wonders what-if."

"So why not step in now?" Ricky asked. "Tell him how you feel. See where it can go. It's not like you don't already know all the things I didn't."

"Because I *do* love him, but not in the way you think. He's my very best friend, and it upsets me to see him sad and hurting. For the longest time, it seemed like he'd never snap out of it. I want him to be happy, and you are the only person I know who has done that recently. He's been different since he met you. He has his spark back. He looks forward to each day, because he knows that he gets to see or talk to you.

"I admit, when he met you, I figured you'd break him again and we'd be left to pick up the pieces. I thought maybe he was making a mistake, and I wanted to tell him to go slow, because the thought of him retreating into his shell again worried me. You didn't though. You made him smile. Don't take that away from him now because you're afraid."

"I don't know…" Ricky hedged as he settled onto the small sofa.

Henley chuckled. "Believe me. You're not the only one who's read romance novels. If you could have seen him two years ago. Hell, six months ago. He sat at that restaurant and mooned over a guy who wouldn't give him the time of day. Then he met this other guy, who told him about corn dogs and opened his eyes to things he's missed out on.

"Don't get me wrong. What he had with Dean? That couldn't have been more real. But they were from the same world. Dean had money. Darwin had his own. But they lived in their own bubble, where it didn't matter. The only thing that made it worthwhile was each other. When Dean got sick, Darwin started to fall apart. When they got the report from the doctor telling Dean his cancer was terminal, they walled themselves off and filled their lives with as much love as they could."

Merlin jumped off Henley's lap, then pounced onto Ricky's. He started stroking the cat, the familiar purr helping to soothe his nerves.

"The night Dean died, Darwin had been at a meeting. Dean knew he wouldn't make it through the night, and he didn't want Darwin to see that, so he forced him to go to the meeting. When Darwin got home, they were putting Dean in an ambulance. He didn't even get to say good-bye, because Dean didn't want the last thing Darwin saw to be the man he loved die."

The tears burned a streak down Ricky's cheeks. "I can't be Dean for him."

"No one wants you to," Henley insisted. "Darwin doesn't want another Dean. He wants you. Let me ask you something. Do you love him?"

Ricky wanted to act indignant. To tell Henley to mind his own business. Instead, he nodded.

"Tonight after he left the restaurant, he stormed away. Told me he would walk back to the office. Even on the night that Dean died, Darwin clung to us for some stability. Right now, though? He's not really all that stable. His brother called me. Darwin wants him to take over the company, because he thinks that if he gives everything away, you'll want to be with him."

"What?" Ricky shouted. "That's crazy."

"Is it? You can't handle him having money, so he's trying to make sure he doesn't have any. It's stupid in my opinion, but in his mind, it's about love. Darwin built Kincade. His parents started the company, but Darwin made it what it is. And he's willing to give that up, to throw it all away, to have a chance with you. Now, tell me that's not worthy of any romance novel you've ever read."

"But...I'm not the guy for him. He's met the president. He could never take me to functions; it would be too embarrassing."

"For you or for him?"

Ricky tilted his head. "What do you mean?"

"What is it that really bothers you about Darwin having money?" Henley leaned forward in the chair, putting his elbows on his knees. "Do you think he'll expect you to change? To become some polished clone of him? He doesn't want that. He wants you."

"I'm just a waiter, but I enjoy it. I don't want to give it up."

Henley stood, walked over to Ricky and put a hand on his shoulder. "Why would you have to?"

"I'm not sure I understand."

"Why would you have to give up something you enjoy? Has he told you he wants you to stay at home? Or that your job would embarrass him?"

Ricky thought for a moment. "No."

"Darwin doesn't believe in changing who you are. He may have the means to give you anything you want, but he knows he can't give you happiness. Only you can do that. If being a waiter is what does that, then be a waiter. I drive a limo, but that's not all that I am. I'm a mechanic. I'm also his best friend." Henley paused for a minute. "Did you read that article about him and the president?"

"No. I saw the picture, and that's what made me realize I couldn't be with him."

"Can you pull it up, please? If it's the one I'm thinking about, you're going to want to see something." Henley grinned.

"You mean there's more?"

"Oh, so much more. Darwin has met with three presidents, several governors, politicians from both sides of the aisle. It's part of what having money does. It opens doors. But it's Darwin who is important to them, not them who is important to him."

139

Ricky grabbed his laptop and opened the page he'd been looking at. He saw the picture of Darwin shaking the president's hand, and his stomach clenched.

"Yes, that's the one," Henley told him. "Did you look closely at that picture?"

"No," Ricky admitted.

"Okay, take a look at the guy on the left in the background."

Ricky let his gaze wander over the picture, and then he noticed what Henley wanted him to see.

"That's you!"

"Yep. Dean couldn't make it, so Dare asked me to go with him. I looked like a pig's ear stuffed into a silk purse, but he didn't care. He introduced me to the president. Did he say, 'this is my driver'? No. He said, 'I'd like you to meet my friend.'

"I wasn't his driver. I wasn't the mechanic who services his car. I was his friend. So tell me, how do you think he'd introduce you? 'This is my waiter?' or do you think he'd say, 'This is my boyfriend.' You're not your job, Ricky. At least not to Darwin. Maria isn't his cook. She's the woman who helped to raise him. Her boys aren't servants. They're the kids he's putting through school. One of them wants to be a doctor. The other hasn't figured out what he wants yet, but Darwin will help him achieve it when he decides.

"It's the same with you. You're the guy he cares for. He doesn't look down on you, so why should you be ashamed?"

His mother had said the same thing to him. He'd told her he wasn't, but in truth, he *was* ashamed. He figured people would think the only reason Darwin was with him would be because Ricky got paid for it. He would never be anything but lower middle class. Even if he got together with Darwin, he'd still only be him.

"What can I offer him?" Ricky asked, wanting to deflect the conversation.

"Something none of us can give him. Your heart. You make him smile, a real, genuine look that none of us has been able to put on his face for so long. But that's not what's bothering you, is it? What's really on your mind?"

He didn't want to say it. The truth would hurt him, but he'd already done the same to Darwin. "I don't want people to look at me differently," he admitted softly.

"Why should you care? Look, I'm not saying that you and Dare will work out. I don't want you to think that. But you'll never know if you run away from him. What's the worst that could happen? You find you're in love with a rich man, and he loves you back? Life isn't a guarantee, Ricky. Darwin and Dean found that out."

Merlin mewed loudly, breaking the tension. Ricky rubbed the cat's ears, eliciting a loud purr. When Ricky looked up at their guest, Henley smiled at him.

"You're a strong guy. If you decide to pursue this relationship and keep being a waiter, Darwin will encourage you to be the very best you can. He will support you in anything you do. Because he wants for you the same thing he wants for the rest of his family: to be happy."

Ricky picked Merlin up and held him to his chest. The cat snuggled in, butting his head against Ricky's chin.

"Is it really that simple?"

"Yep. It really is. Or you can go ahead and continue to make it difficult. It's up to you how this is going to play out. You have the power here."

Ricky thought about Darwin, and his heart still fluttered when the image of the man came to mind.

"I've been stupid," he admitted.

"I can't deny that," Henley replied, smirking.

"He'd really give it all up to be with me?"

"Kent said he called the lawyers to draft the paperwork. What does that tell you?"

No one had ever been willing to give something up for Ricky, especially not something they'd spent most of their life building. The thought that Darwin would sacrifice so much enflamed Ricky. Equal parts love and anger warred for dominance as he realized how unfair he'd been. He hadn't even given Darwin—given *them*—a fair chance. He had been so protective of his own feelings, he'd never given a thought to the man he believed he loved.

"I need to go see him."

"Yeah, you really do. If you don't want to be with him, then explain your reasons. Don't just say we're not right for each other. That's not fair to him at all. Whether you know it or not, he's fully vested in you."

Ricky stood, dislodging a mewing Merlin. "Thanks for coming by."

"You want a ride? I happen to know there's a limo parked outside."

"You left the limo out there? Unattended? Oh God, I hope to hell you have tires when we get out there."

Henley laughed. Then his expression turned hopeful. "So you'll go see him?"

"I will."

After they got into the car, Henley explained to Ricky that Kent had called him after the meeting with Darwin. He'd been concerned and wanted to know what Henley knew. He said that he and his wife didn't want the company, but they would take it to keep it from being sold off or the employees put out of work.

"I don't think Darwin's really giving this the thought he needs to," Henley said. "Even after Dean died, he still fought to keep the company going. Those are his people, and he'd give his right arm before he let anything happen to them."

Ricky couldn't help but be humbled. No one, aside from his mother and sister, had ever put him first.

"I've been a dick," he said quietly.

"So has Darwin. He didn't want to tell you who he was, because he wanted you to see the person, not the money."

"Money changes everything."

"Exactly. Dare's parents drilled that into his head from the time he was old enough to earn an allowance. You always had to be careful about people, because when they found out you had money, they usually only saw you as a potential stepping stone."

"I'd never do that."

"But you did. Only in reverse. You looked at the money and saw it as something to keep you apart. You stopped seeing Darwin and only saw dollar signs."

"Because I don't want his money!"

"That's fine. Earn your own. He won't mind. Darwin wants you happy. Preferably with him, of course. If the money aspect bothers you that much, tell him. The two of you will have to deal with it. Pretty sure it won't go away."

Henley spoke the truth. Darwin's money wouldn't go away if he could help it. He loved Darwin, and he understood that he wouldn't be happy if he gave everything up. He didn't want Darwin to resent him.

Henley parked the car and then walked Ricky to the door. When a man opened the door, Henley shook his hand. "Hey, Mitch. This is Ricky. He's here to see Darwin."

"After his brother left, he told me he didn't want to be disturbed."

"Trust me on this one, Dare will want to see Ricky."

He could see Mitch mulling it over. "Okay. But only because I know you. I hope Mr. Kincade is okay. He didn't seem himself when he came in."

"Don't worry," Ricky promised, "he'll be better after we talk."

"I'll leave you to it," Henley said. "Just be careful, okay?"

"Promise."

Henley handed Ricky a card with his number on it. "In case you need me, give me a call. I don't think I'll be able to sleep tonight anyway."

Henley left after he keyed Ricky into the private elevator. Ricky took a couple of breaths while he ascended to the floor that held

Darwin's office. As he stepped off the elevator, he noticed the dimmed lights, and the ungodly snores that came from somewhere in the room. He flicked on the light switch and saw Darwin asleep on the couch, a nearly empty bottle of Macallan M on the floor next to him.

"Fuck," Ricky whispered.

He knelt down next to the extra-wide couch and put a hand on Darwin's shoulder.

"Hey, wake up, Darwin."

Darwin snorted, then rolled over.

"Darwin? I need to talk to you."

Darwin's eyes popped open. He gazed unsteadily at Ricky, then groaned.

"I really fucked up," he said, then belched. "I thought I could have it all, but after a while, I realized all I really wanted was Ricky."

Ricky stroked Darwin's forehead. "I'm Ricky. You can talk with me."

A shake of his head turned out to be the only answer Ricky got. He chuckled.

"Okay, how about if we talk in the morning?"

He nudged Darwin over on the couch, then lay beside him, an arm wrapped protectively around his waist. "I'm sorry I was such an ass," he said, kissing Darwin's neck.

"I love you, Ricky."

Ricky snuggled in closer. "I love you, too, Darwin."

CHAPTER THIRTEEN

Darwin's mouth felt dry and gummy. He'd known as soon as he'd pulled the bottle out that he shouldn't do it, but he needed to forget. At least for a while. Today he'd pay for it. His head already wanted to burst, and his stomach heaved at the thought of moving. He closed his eyes, soaking up the warmth surrounding him.

His eyes flew open, and he jerked up, groaning at his mistake.

"Damn," he whimpered.

"Where do you keep the aspirin?" a sleepy voice beside him asked.

Darwin looked down and blinked several times, trying to clear the hallucination from his mind.

"Really here, Darwin," Ricky said, amusement in his voice.

"But how? Wait. Let me guess. Henley."

"He came to see me last night. We talked. I want to apologize to you for not believing in you. In us. It all happened so fast, and I wasn't prepared. If you're willing, I'd like us to start over."

"We can't," Darwin groaned.

"Why not?" Ricky asked, pulling Darwin back down on the couch.

"I don't want to start over. I acted stupid, and I don't want to do it again."

"Okay, how about this then? My name is Ricky. I'm a waiter."

Darwin chuckled. "I'm Darwin. I own Kincade International. At least I did. I asked Kent to take over the company last night."

"Wanna tell me why?"

"Because I wanted to be the guy you could love. If my having money got in the way, then it seemed a simple solution. But…"

"But?"

Darwin sighed. "But it's not. After Kent left, I got drunk, and it gave me great clarity. I can't change who I am, Ricky. Not even for you."

"I don't want you to," Ricky replied forcefully. "Do you want *me* to change for you?"

Darwin tried to sit up, but Ricky held him in place.

"No. That's what I wanted you to understand. I want you however you want to be. If you want to be a waiter, then be a waiter. What were you going to school for?"

"Restaurant management," Ricky answered. "One day I'd like to open my own place." He laughed. "I'll need a good chef. Maybe I'll steal Maria away to come cook for me."

"Over my dead body." His stomach lurched, and Darwin groaned. "Which may not be far off."

Ricky laughed, then kissed Darwin's neck. "Can I make a suggestion?"

"Please. As long as you do it quietly."

"How about if we take the time to get to know one another properly? No more hiding, no more doubts."

"I'd like that," Darwin admitted. "Can I start by confessing something to you?"

"Sure."

"I love being held."

"Good, because I like holding you."

They lay there until the office began to fill with sunlight. Ricky got up, drew the blinds, then snuggled up against Darwin again.

"I've got to talk to Kent," Darwin said. "I need to see if he'll forgive me when I ask him not to take the company."

"He called Henley last night to talk you out of it. I don't think he'll be too upset."

"Really? Hmm. The best thing about people is how they constantly surprise you. It used to be that Kent wanted the company, but now that he has his own, he's grown into it."

"And he's your brother, so he loves you."

"That may be part of it," Darwin conceded. "I'll still have to contact the lawyers, and see if I can undo some of the damage I caused last night."

"Is there anything I can do to help?" Ricky asked, sitting up.

"Just promise me you're really here. I think the idea that you're only an illusion would likely kill me."

Ricky stood, leaned over, and put a hand on the back of Darwin's neck to pull him up into a kiss. When they separated, Darwin felt a huge weight being lifted from him.

"Please tell me we'll really try to make this work."

"We're really going to try. I'm not saying it'll be easy. I'm still nervous at how people will look at me. Poor student, rich man. Oh, he must be sleeping with him for his money."

"You know what I say to that? Fuck them. We know the truth, and that's all that matters."

"I'll try to keep that in mind. But I may need you to remind me on occasion."

"As often as you need," Darwin promised.

While Darwin made his phone calls, first to his relieved lawyer, then to his brother, he watched Ricky as he cleaned up the mess Darwin had made of the office. He liked seeing him here, and the urge to get him back down on the couch nearly overwhelmed him. But he said they'd take it slowly, and he'd honor that.

It had just passed noon when he finished the last of the phone calls. Darwin was grateful it was Saturday, because otherwise, Heather would have been in his office, instead of Ricky.

"You were right. Everyone did seem happy that I changed my mind." He went back to the couch and took a seat.

"Can you blame them? Henley explained to me that you're the heart of the company. These people depend on you, and probably would panic if you sold it."

Darwin shook his head at his own stupidity. He'd have to calm the staff if any word of this leaked out. Fortunately, he didn't think it would, but that really hadn't been the point. He'd messed up big time. First with Ricky by trying to be someone he wasn't, then with his staff by wanting to be someone else completely.

"I'm sorry about everything. I should have been upfront with you from the beginning. But I liked bringing you dinner, and the look on your face when you saw it. It felt nice to just be Darwin for a while."

Ricky smiled and took Darwin's hand.

"I get it. I really do. This job comes with a lot of stress. People always wanting something from you. And I have to admit, having you bring me corn dogs? That had to be the coolest gift ever. I barely had enough money in my account to pay off my loans and keep a roof over my head. So a meal with you lifted my spirits."

The offer of help was once more on the tip of Darwin's tongue, but he had no idea how Ricky would respond. But they'd promised to try, and Darwin needed to ask the question on his mind if they were going to make a go of it.

"Okay, I have to ask. If we're going to see how this works, what am I allowed to do? I don't want to pressure you or make you uncomfortable, so you have to give me some guidelines."

Ricky's fingers trailed over Darwin's neck.

"You can hug me. Kiss me. Hold me. Buy me dinner on occasion, as long as I can return the favor. Keep in mind that I might not be able to afford some of the places you'd probably go to, though."

"What if I wanted to offer to help to pay off your student loans?"

"No," Ricky said adamantly, then his voice softened. "At least not now. I want us to take the time to know each other. The real us. I need that before I accept any offer of assistance. Does that make sense?"

It did. The fact Ricky said it filled Darwin with pride. Ricky had proven Darwin's parents right. Money does change everything. Sometimes it shows you a person's true character.

***

Ricky couldn't complain at all about the new pace of their relationship. Darwin wanted to take it slower, to really get to know each other. They'd already done fast, but slow? He guessed that worked, too. The only problem came when they went back to their own places. Ricky saw his apartment in a new light. It had no warmth, not like Darwin. He missed the man more than he'd ever thought he could. It seemed slow had a downside, too.

One evening, Darwin told Ricky he had to attend a function for Kincade. Ricky said he understood, and told his lover he'd see him later in the week.

"But…that's not why I'm telling you. I want you to come with me."

"You what? But—"

"No buts. Come with me," Darwin pleaded. "Show everyone you're not embarrassed to be seen with me. Show *me*."

Ricky couldn't believe this man would think it was Ricky who was embarrassed. He smiled at Darwin and said, "I'd love to," even if his insides quivered.

So together they went out and bought Ricky a tuxedo. He had to admit, it looked really good on him. When Darwin came to pick him up, Henley opened the door to the limo and gave Ricky a wink and a smile.

"Don't be nervous," Darwin told him as Henley drove them to the event. "This is a small function, and I promise I won't leave your side the whole night, unless you ask me to."

"I don't think you need to worry about that," Ricky grumbled.

Ricky's nerves never calmed. The moment they walked into the room, all eyes were on them. He felt like a bug in a jar. It got even worse when he saw who had come in and made a beeline toward them.

"That's the governor," Ricky whispered, desperately trying to quell the panic.

"Yeah," Darwin replied. "Nice guy. Needs to work on his golf game, though. Hey, do you play golf?"

Ricky frowned. "Oh, hell no."

Darwin smiled. "Well, if you ever want to learn, I'll teach you," he whispered as the governor reached them.

"Darwin, nice to see you again," the governor said, his hand extended.

Darwin gripped the man's hand and smiled. "Good to see you, too, Bob. And you look lovely tonight, Estelle."

The governor's wife blushed, and shook Darwin's hand.

"Governor, Estelle, I'd like to introduce you to my date for this evening. This is Ricky Donnelly. Ricky, Governor and Mrs. Mills."

Ricky stood awestruck. When Darwin gave his hand a squeeze, he shook his head. "Sorry. Just not used to being at one of these events." Then he wiped his sweaty palm on his pants leg and shook hands with their governor.

"It's a pleasure, Ricky. Glad you could make it. Do you work with Darwin?"

Ricky had no idea what to say. Fortunately, Darwin stepped up to save him.

"He's a waiter at Rossi's. Probably their best one."

His jaw dropped when Darwin said that. What surprised him more was when the governor replied, "My wife and I took our family there last year. Great food and really wonderful service. Maybe we'll see you there one day."

Someone waved at them from across the room, and the governor groaned. "Time to put on my game face. Ricky, Darwin, good to see you both."

As they walked away, Ricky gaped at Darwin. "You told them who I was."

"What? Didn't you want me to?"

Ricky shrugged. "I just didn't think you would."

A warm hand slid across Ricky's cheek. "I told you, I am not ashamed of you or what you do for a living. Let me ask you something, and I want you to be honest. When you came to my office that night, do you remember the name of the man who let you in?"

Ricky had to think back to that night almost a month ago.

"Mitch," he replied.

"Exactly. Now, tell me, how is Mitch any less important to Kincade than anyone else? Even me? I loved my parents, but they saw class division. They would have had a stroke if they'd known Henley and I were friends, because they thought the chauffeur's son was beneath us. I disagreed. Without Henley, life would have been very lonely."

Ricky pondered what Darwin meant. "So you really don't care I'm only a waiter."

"I never cared. What you do is a job, it's not who you are. I own Kincade, but it's not who I am. I'm Darwin, lover of corn dogs, raspberry nebula shakes, and waiters with green eyes."

He pulled Ricky to him, and slanted his mouth over Ricky's, in front of the governor and everyone. If Ricky needed proof of Darwin's love, he got it in spades. They'd kissed before, but not like this. Ricky could only call it being claimed. With that one kiss, Darwin let him know the depth of his feelings, and they shook Ricky to his core.

"Can we go home?" Ricky whispered, running a hand over Darwin's chest.

"Yes, please," Darwin whimpered.

They thanked the hosts, said good night, and headed for the limo. Henley stood there, chatting with another driver who gave him a bright smile. When he noticed them, Henley told the man he'd call, then opened the door. Darwin and Ricky tumbled into the backseat, not wanting to stop touching one another.

"Guess I'll introduce Jeff to you later," Henley said. He chuckled as the privacy screen rose.

Ricky wished for more hands as he touched Darwin anywhere he could. He'd waited for this night and had been astounded at their patience. But tonight he wanted Darwin. To finally come together in a way that solidified their relationship.

He barely noticed when they'd gotten back to his apartment. Darwin opened the door before Henley could even get out of the car, then pulled him to the elevator. As soon as the door opened and Ricky pushed his floor, Darwin pinned him against the wall.

"You smell so good," he moaned. "Been wanting to touch you all night. I kept seeing people checking you out, even though they knew you were there with me."

"People were looking at me?" Ricky asked self-consciously.

"They wanted you. The man who dazzled everyone with his charm. The one with the strength of character to match the amazing body. And I laughed, because you didn't even notice them. You only looked at me."

They got into Ricky's apartment, and for the first time, Darwin got to meet Merlin, who greeted him at the door with a loud whine.

"Feeding time," Ricky explained. "Better than an alarm clock."

"Can I feed him?"

The question warmed Ricky. He showed Darwin where he kept the food, then stood back and watched as Merlin tried to climb Darwin's leg while he filled the dish. When Darwin put the food down, Merlin forgot all about them.

"It's a cat thing," Ricky explained. "Merlin thinks he's a dog, at least until feeding time. But I really don't want to talk about that right now."

He took Darwin by the hand and led him to the bedroom. A few weeks ago, he would have been embarrassed for Darwin to see the place, but he now understood the man simply didn't see the world in that way.

They made short work of their clothes, then climbed onto the bed. Ricky hadn't seen Darwin naked before, and the sight took his breath away. He had a furry chest and stomach, with a thin line of hair that ran down to his groin. Not overly muscled, he still possessed a nice body that Ricky couldn't wait to explore. But that would wait until he had a few more kisses.

He leaned forward and nibbled on Darwin's neck, interspersing the touch with quick nips to the kiss-swollen lips. Darwin groaned, thrusting up. Ricky wrapped a hand around Darwin's cock, loving the weight of it.

"Ricky, please…" Darwin pleaded.

"What? What's wrong?"

"No one has touched me for years," Darwin admitted. "It feels too good, and I'm going to come if you keep doing that."

Ricky laughed. "You make it sound like that's not the goal."

"Oh, God. I want to come. But I want it while you're inside me."

That brought Ricky up short. His hands stopped moving, and he could barely breathe. "You want me to…?"

"Don't be so surprised. I love you and I want you to love me back. I like to bottom. I prefer it, in fact. But I haven't in a long while. Please be patient."

Ricky gazed into Darwin's eyes and smiled. "I will. And I promise I'm going to do my best to make it good for you."

He stroked a hand down Darwin's chest, loving the sounds that came from the man. It sounded almost like purring.

"You're so needy," he teased.

"I haven't been with anyone since Dean," Darwin confessed.

And here the man lay, willing to share his body with Ricky. Though he claimed to want it, Ricky noticed the goose bumps that dotted Darwin's arms.

"Hey, it's okay. We don't have to do this," Ricky assured him.

"Shut up. I've been waiting for this. I've dreamed about it. You don't know what you do to me. You burn me up every time you touch me. When we're out on the dance floor, I expect to go up in flames at any moment. Yeah, I'm nervous, but I need to see if the reality is going to be as good as the dream."

"So, no pressure?"

Darwin grinned. "I love you."

As he ran his fingertips over Darwin's stomach, he noticed his lover spread his legs a little. He had to be as eager as Ricky. They'd danced around sex since they'd gotten together, making kissing and a little groping be enough. But now, Darwin wanted him. And he wanted Ricky to... God, he never expected that. But now that he knew what made him happy, he'd never let Darwin go.

He stroked his fingers across Darwin's shaft, which jerked and did a little dance.

"Fuck. Stop teasing."

"Not," Ricky assured him. "Savoring."

He wrapped his hand around Darwin's shaft and gave it a few good tugs. Darwin writhed on the bed.

"So good," he cried out. "Please. I'll do anything. Just touch me."

Tears ran down Darwin's cheeks. Ricky leaned over and licked one of them. "I'm not going to leave you wanting. I swear."

He pulled Darwin's legs open, then reached into his nightstand for the economy-sized bottle of lube he'd gotten plenty of use from since he and Darwin had met. Fumbling around in the drawer, he found a lone condom that still retained freshness. He gently tore it open and laid the packet on the bed. Snapping the lid of the lube, he put a dab on his index finger and slowly ran it over Darwin's pucker. His head shook side to side, and a deep moan escaped as Ricky dipped the tip of his finger into Darwin's ass.

"Oh, God," Darwin gasped. "Fuck, I've missed this."

Ricky grinned and let a small trail of lubricant drizzle down Darwin's crack, then he spread it around. He slipped his finger inside, marveling at the heat. He had to wonder if he put his cock inside Darwin, would he last beyond the initial stroke?

"More, please," Darwin pleaded.

"When I'm ready," Ricky replied. "I won't hurt you, so you've got to be patient."

When he slipped the finger in again, Darwin thrust up, trying to drive the digit deeper. Ricky grinned at how enthusiastic and hungry for affection Darwin was. He added another finger, making sure he moved slowly. He'd been serious when he told Darwin he had no desire to hurt him. And since Ricky didn't have all that much experience, he needed to keep an eye on Darwin for any discomfort.

"So good," Darwin murmured. "Please, don't stop."

The encouragement spurred him on, as did the absolute rapture of Darwin's expression. He pushed in a third finger, mesmerized by how Darwin's body responded to him, gripping him tight.

He removed his fingers, and Darwin whimpered.

"Shhh. Almost time," Ricky said quietly. He slipped the condom over his engorged cock, then added a little more lube. He slid between Darwin's legs and hoisted his knees. The slick shined in the light, and Ricky swallowed.

With one hand guiding him, he put his cock against Darwin's hole and pushed gently. Darwin grunted.

"Am I hurting you?" Ricky asked, ready to stop.

"A little burn, but it'll go away. Just…go slow, okay?"

Ricky gave a slight thrust of his hips, burying himself deeper into Darwin's channel. Darwin lay there, his head thrown back, mouth open as Ricky bottomed out.

"That's all of it," he said. "You took all of me."

Darwin looked up and grinned. "There was quite a bit to take. Just hold still and let me get used to it, okay?"

He watched as Darwin's expression went from a pinched look to one of acceptance, and, finally, one of pure pleasure. Ricky pulled out slightly, then pushed back in. He repeated the motion, drawing out a little more each time, then punching in a little harder.

"Yes, like that," Darwin mewled. "I won't break, I promise."

Ricky pushed Darwin's legs back, leaving him wide open, and began to slam in as hard as he could. He'd known the sensations would be indescribable, but this was beyond his imagining. Darwin cried out as come shot from his cock, coating his belly and chest. His ass muscles clenched, gripping Ricky, demanding their prize. When Ricky came, he cried out how much he loved Darwin. How much he'd always love him.

Then he collapsed on top of his lover, claiming his mouth in a kiss.

"Stay with me," Darwin begged. "I don't want to be alone anymore."

Any fear Ricky had of losing himself evaporated. All he felt now was love.

"Okay," he agreed.

"Really?"

"Yeah. But you know I come with a cat."

"And he's welcome, too. As long as you're there, we can have as many cats as you want."

"How about, after a shower, we try for round two?"

"I'm all in."

Ricky knew Darwin meant he'd be there for the long haul.

"Me, too," he promised.

Ricky moved into the mansion a few days later. Darwin, Henley, Tomás, and Martín came to help him load up his apartment. It didn't take long. Ricky directed them to throw most of his furniture onto the curb, but Darwin hedged.

"You don't want any of this?"

Ricky gazed longingly at his chair. He loved it, even though it had gone threadbare in some places, and Merlin had taken to scratching the leg of it. But none of this stuff would fit in a mansion.

"No, it's fine."

"Could you guys excuse us for a minute?"

Darwin took Ricky's elbow and led him into the bedroom where they'd made love. "Why don't you want your stuff?"

Ricky glanced down at his feet. "You probably have that Chippendale stuff in your house. I don't think a chair from a thrift store is going to cut it."

Darwin scrubbed a hand over his face.

"You know, one day you *will* understand. I want you as you are—chair, cat, and all. If you want to redo the mansion with everything from a thrift store, that's perfectly fine. We won't be living in a museum. It's going to be our home. And it's going to be as much yours as it is mine."

Ricky blinked back the tears. "You really mean that, don't you?"

Darwin pulled Ricky into a tight hug. "Of course I do. We can put the old stuff into storage and redecorate it together if you want."

"No, that's fine. But…could I have somewhere to put my chair? I really love that thing."

"Anywhere you want," Darwin promised, a smile blooming over his face. He kissed the tip of Ricky's nose. "Now, come on, Maria is making you a welcome home dinner tonight, and we're all looking forward to celebrating."

That night they toasted Ricky with champagne and Maria made him his favorite meal—chicken and dumplings.

"How did you know?" he said, digging in.

"Your mother and I talk. She's got some funny stories. I especially like the one about you and the juice box."

Ricky groaned and dipped his chin to his chest.

"She also asked me to tell you that she and I were going shopping together next week."

Ricky threw his hands in the air. "Oh, God. Kill me now."

Maria walked over, bent down, and kissed his cheek. "Don't worry, *niño*, I promise it will all be okay."

A few nights later, Darwin met Ricky at the door when he came home from work. He was dressed in jeans and a T-shirt, and looked absolutely amazing.

"Ready?"

"For?"

"We're going out."

Ricky frowned. "Another event?"

"Not this time. Alexander put some clothes out for you. Hurry up and get dressed."

Ricky trudged up the stairs to their bedroom and found a pair of skintight jeans for him, along with a green shirt Darwin loved. He knew now what his lover had planned, and he was all for it.

The trip to the bar was quick, or maybe it just seemed that way, because he and Darwin were making out in the back of the limo. When Henley opened the door, the two of them almost fell out, which Henley found absolutely hilarious.

Darwin glared at him. "Go home. We can call when we're done."

Henley flushed, rubbed the back of his head and gave a sheepish grin. "Actually, can you grab a cab? I have a date."

Darwin grinned. "Oh? Do tell."

"Jeff and I are going out to dinner."

Darwin gave his oldest, dearest friend a smile. "I'm so glad. Just tell him to have you home by midnight."

Henley waggled his brows. "With a little luck, I'll be staying there for breakfast."

They all laughed, then Henley got in the car and drove off, leaving Ricky and Darwin outside the club they'd gone to on their first semi-date.

"I didn't think you'd want to come back here," Ricky admitted.

"Are you kidding? I love the ale, and the dancing part wasn't half bad. Plus, I may want to try something new." He winked.

They drank, laughed, and had an amazing time. Darwin rose from the table, and Ricky knew what idea had popped into his lover's head.

"Again? We just did it. I might need a break."

Darwin scoffed. "Five whole minutes. I can't believe you are going to claim exhaustion after five minutes."

"I worked tonight," Ricky protested. "And I ran my ass off."

"Come on," Darwin whined. "One little dance."

He grabbed Ricky's hand and pulled him onto the dance floor of the club that, if Darwin liked it, would likely become their Friday night haunt. Ricky kicked himself for thinking Darwin wouldn't fit in this world. It had taken him time to relax, but once he had, Ricky found Darwin enjoyed being up on the floor with him, touching each other, and falling in love all over again.

EPILOGUE

Three months later

"Hurry up, Darwin. They'll be here any minute!" Ricky shouted.

Darwin came down the stairs and his heart beat a little faster when he found Ricky standing next to the Christmas tree they'd decorated. He seemed entranced by the thousands of lights shimmering off the pile of gifts that lay beneath it. Eighteen feet tall, the tree nearly touched the ceiling of the great room.

They'd gathered together the day before to decorate it. He'd loved watching as Maria and her kids; Henley and his boyfriend, Jeff; Alexander, the butler; Cynthia, the laundress; Kyle, the groundskeeper; and Nathan, the household manager, had gotten together with Ricky's mom, as well as Trish and her family to decorate the tree. They'd laughed, drunk eggnog, and had a great time in each other's company.

Tonight they were going to get together again to celebrate their first Christmas as a family. It would be the largest gathering the house had seen since Dean was still alive. Darwin swallowed hard. He and Ricky had talked about Dean, and to his surprise, Ricky insisted that the portrait of Dean that had been stored away be present for the holiday. He glanced up at the picture and smiled. Dean would have wished him and Ricky nothing but happiness.

The doorbell rang. Alexander opened it for their first guests. Megan and Trish, along with Trish's husband, Jack, and their two kids, Mitchell and Deanna, had come in, dressed for the season in matching red and green sweaters. Darwin and Ricky walked over to greet them after Alexander had taken their coats.

Ricky's mom glowed with pride as he stood by Darwin, arm wrapped around him.

"The two of you are so cute together," she gushed.

"We are, aren't we?" Ricky teased.

Ricky took his family into the kitchen with a promise of Maria's homemade Christmas cookies, which the kids seemed especially excited about, while Darwin waited for their other guests.

They trickled in over the next hour. Darwin welcomed his former executive assistant, Heather, who had been promoted to their Human Resources manager, as well as Dylan Simons, his new assistant who seemed like Heather on steroids. Where she was efficient, Dylan strived to be hyper-efficient. Darwin had to remind him that the office would be closed, and even then the young man wanted to go in to catch up on work. The only way he could be certain Dylan wouldn't go in was to invite him to the party. The last to arrive, much to Darwin's surprise, had been Jeff Tan, Henley's boyfriend and former driver for Eric Tremaine, who had been a friend of Dean's.

Henley had been dating the man for several months now, and they seemed very much in tune with one another. When his friend saw Jeff, he rushed over, hugged him and gave him a kiss.

"So glad you made it," Henley gushed.

"Thank you for inviting me, Mr. Kincade."

Darwin held out his hand. "Darwin, please."

Ricky came back from the kitchen and directed his family to take a seat in the great room. Jeff and Henley followed them, Jeff accepting a glass of eggnog from his boyfriend.

Henley had whispered something to Jeff, kissed him again, then strode over to Darwin and Ricky. "Hey, Dare? Can I borrow the two of you for a minute?"

Darwin shrugged. "I guess."

They went into the kitchen, checked the mulled cider, added a dash of brandy to it, and then all sat at the table, Ricky sitting to Darwin's left.

"I see you and Jeff are getting pretty serious," Ricky said.

Henley blushed. The first time Darwin had seen him with Jeff…when he actually had been introduced, and not worrying about getting to Ricky's house, had been a very welcome surprise. And watching them together, it made Darwin think that it wouldn't be long before his friend asked about Jeff living with him. He couldn't wait for that day.

"We are. It's…different. We talked about taking things slow, but they're moving at their own pace. I really like him."

Darwin gave two seconds thought to teasing Henley, then decided against it. His friend deserved happiness, too. "So, what did you want to talk to us about?"

Henley smiled. "I hope that there isn't a gift beneath the tree for me."

"What?" Darwin snapped. "That's silly. Why wouldn't—"

"I've got mine already," Henley continued, ignoring Darwin's outburst. "After Dean died, there was something missing in the house. We all pretended it hadn't left, but it did. He took the life and love with him. We existed, and clung to one another, because we needed to. But when Ricky came into your life—into *our* lives— everything seemed to click back into place.

"I don't want this to sound sappy, honest, but being here now is like coming back together as a family, and we have Ricky to thank for that. You've opened up the remaining wings, hired new staff to start after the new year. The house is going to be alive again."

Ricky's fingers clenched under the table, and a startling blush crept up his cheeks.

"I'm not sure what to say," Ricky admitted. "I thought I wouldn't fit in here. I figured Darwin would come to his senses, and we'd go our separate ways. But every night we sit in front of the fire, cup of Maria's hot cocoa in hand, and we just talk about our days. He listens when I tell him about the parties I served, how grateful I am he helped me to pay off my student loans, and how proud I am to have him in my life. He smiles at me, then we talk about his day."

And Ricky had loved everything they'd discussed, because it made him more comfortable in his expanded family. Things like how Kent had surprised him when he said the new product would be made available to anyone who wanted it. Those who couldn't afford it would be able to get one through a special fund that had been set up to help low-income families. And larger versions were being offered in partnership with smaller towns because it was something KK's team could do to give back to the community. The best part, at least for Ricky, was when Darwin told him Kent said it might not be the moneymaker he'd envisioned, but the resulting PR had others coming forward to invest in new projects Kent and his team had come up with. Also, his wife, Mila, had stood up with him at their last board meeting, and called up the people who had made it possible, and said how proud she was of the changes he'd made in their lives. Ricky doubted he could be happier about the new direction his life had taken, and that he finally realized it.

Ricky sighed, and folded his hands in front of him on the table. "I'm sorry it took me so long to figure out how much I wanted—needed—to be here."

Everyone stayed quiet for a few moments. Then Darwin clapped his hands and smiled. "Okay, enough of this. We've got guests who've got gifts to open."

The three men went back to the great room, where everyone sat near the fireplace. Darwin and Ricky slid into an open spot on the couch, while Henley sat on the floor between Jeff's legs.

"Do we want to wait for Kent and Mila?" Ricky asked.

Darwin considered it for a moment. "No. They'll be by for dinner. I don't want to make anyone suffer if they can't open their presents."

Martín and Tomás had the decency to at least appear sheepish, but they didn't take their eyes of the stack of gifts that bore their names.

"You can open one, *niños*," Maria chided.

They dug in the pile and pulled out the two biggest packages. Wrapping paper flew as they yanked it off the boxes. When they saw the two new Mac computers, they turned toward Darwin, their expressions a joy to see. They launched themselves at him, thanking him for the gift. Then they jumped on Ricky, hugging him, and saying, "Thank you, Uncle Ricky."

Ricky seemed shell-shocked, like he'd just realized that he belonged in the family, too. He didn't hesitate to accept the hugs.

After the boys ran to their rooms to put the new computers to use, Ricky handed his mother and sister a small box each.

"So the boys get a computer, and we get matchbooks," Megan teased. When they opened the boxes, though, their breath caught.

"Ooh. This is gorgeous," Trish exclaimed, pulling out a bracelet dotted with sapphires."

"It's platinum," Ricky told them, helping his mother latch it around her wrist. "I don't want either of you having your skin turn green."

Megan clutched him to her. "Oh, thank you both so much, honey. It's beautiful." She kissed him on the cheek, which had Ricky's smile a mile wide.

Darwin grinned. "It's all Ricky. My gift to you is still under the tree. But it's going to pale in comparison to that."

Ricky preened a little. Darwin knew how proud he'd been when he saved up enough money to buy the gifts. He realized it was something his lover wanted to do on his own, and he'd told him that if he wanted help, he only needed to say so. Ricky hadn't, though. He'd worked extra shifts at Rossi's to make sure he could afford what his mother had asked for, even if it had only been her teasing him.

The fact Ricky had done this on his own showed his fierce independent streak, and hadn't upset Darwin at all. While he wanted to give Ricky everything, he knew that sometimes—not always—he'd want to show he could do things himself. And that was okay with him.

Ricky caught his attention and gave Darwin a wink and mouthed 'I love you.'

****

The great room had been covered in wrapping paper, ribbons, and assorted boxes. Everyone laughed as Merlin dove into the paper, winding his way through it, his head popping up at intervals to make sure people were watching. Eventually Ricky picked the cat up and teased him with a ribbon until his furry friend fell asleep next to him.

It looked every bit a family celebration, and Ricky couldn't help but feel proud to be part of it. He let his gaze wander over those who had come, and his heart felt full to bursting. Kent and Mila had shown up, arms laden with gifts, and had been absorbed into the throng of guests. His mother and sister had fallen asleep in front of the fire, their bracelets reflecting the dancing flames. Jack had taken the kids and put them to bed in one of the guest rooms. Darwin had said that Heather had been doing her best to keep Dylan occupied, because he seemed lost without work to do. Ricky hoped the young man worked out as Darwin's assistant, because he seemed sweet. And the last time he'd seen Henley was hours ago when the man had Jeff under the mistletoe.

Ricky looked around the room at the people who now made up his family and wondered once again why he'd been so resistant. Why he'd denied his feelings, even though doing so hurt him deeply. Darwin hadn't tried once to control him or make him feel as though he were the lesser partner. On the contrary, he'd gone out of his way to encourage Ricky. To give him a push when he thought it necessary, but backing off when he could see Ricky had things under control.

Since he'd moved into the mansion, Darwin had set him up with an office, shelves loaded with books on running your own restaurant, computers, and even an on-call advisor to help him. Ricky had initially chafed, but his mother reminded him that we allowed the ones we loved to help when they could. Ricky listened—finally—to what she had to say and threw himself into studies. With the help of the company Darwin set up to assist him, he learned more than he ever had at school.

Darwin had gone off to help the boys, who were having a problem setting up the new computers. Maria had snuck off to the kitchen to check on their dinner. When Darwin had told her they could have the whole thing catered, she'd smacked him upside the head and told him he should never say such things to her. He'd wrapped her in a hug and kissed her cheek, which had made her giggle like a schoolgirl.

"Darwin?" Maria called. "Dinner will be ready in ten minutes. Do you think it's time?"

With a grin, Darwin came in from the other room, both boys in tow. They were decked out in white tuxedos, and each of Maria's sons carried a small silver tray with a domed lid atop it.

"What's this?" Ricky demanded.

"Your gift, of course."

He looked down at the watch Darwin had given him. A high-end, scratch-resistant, accurate to a second every millennium thing, with more bells and whistles than a whole fleet of space shuttles, or so Tomás had explained as Ricky had slipped it onto his wrist. Then he and his brother had said how they'd helped to pick it out, which gave Ricky a laugh.

"This is my gift."

"Nah, that's just a distraction. These are your gifts."

Martín went first. He held out the silver tray, removing the lid with flair. Ricky saw that it contained an envelope. He couldn't imagine why, but his nerves jangled. He opened the gift, and his jaw dropped.

"I'm not sure I understand," he exclaimed.

"You are now the proud owner of Asiago. Or, whatever you choose to name it."

"But...you can't."

166

"Oh, yeah, I can," Darwin said smugly. He dropped the pitch of his voice and did a very bad Godfather imitation. "I made Berkhardt an offer he couldn't refuse."

Everyone cracked up, and after they'd settled down, Ricky turned to Darwin and asked, "Why?"

Darwin cupped Ricky's cheek. "Because he fired the best waiter that the place had. And he treats his employees like crap. Asiago may have the finest reputation in town, but they have—well, had—a bully for an owner. I sat down with him and gave him an offer. His eyes bugged out, and he signed it over a few days later. Now the place is in your name. Make something wonderful out of it. If you need help, Louisa is still there. Though I did find out from Berkhardt that he'd intended to eliminate her. Something about her countermanding him once too often."

Ricky laughed, despite the shock he felt. Who gave a restaurant as a gift?

"I suppose you can do that when you're a billionaire," he said, detecting a hint of bitterness in his tone.

"Wait. What? Oh, no. You don't understand. You own the restaurant, but I'm giving it to you as sort of a pay-as-you-go kind of thing. You'll find the payment plan and interest rates are very reasonable."

Ricky reached up and pulled Darwin down on the couch. "Explain."

"I know you well enough by now that no matter how much I wanted to give it to you, you'd feel you needed to earn it. And you will." He paused for a moment. "I'm hoping that one day you'll be able to accept a gift when I give it to you. But until you're ready, we'll figure it out. As for the restaurant, this is going to be a lot of work. I'm certain you're up to the challenge, though."

Tears pricked the corners of Ricky's eyes. Darwin believed in him, and he'd always known it. But now? This? Ricky knew he could never have opened his own restaurant without help. He'd planned on talking to the bank, but with no collateral, no background beyond school, they'd have laughed at him. Darwin had handed him a golden opportunity to prove himself.

Tomás held out the second tray.

"I'm scared," Ricky admitted. The man had given him a restaurant. What could possibly be left to give?

He took the cover from the tray and discovered a ring box. The enormity of what lay inside hit him hard. He opened it with shaky hands, to find a plain silver band inside.

"This isn't an engagement ring," Darwin told him hastily. "I want to wait on that until we're both in a good spot. You'll be really busy for a while, and I'm going to back you. For now, I guess you could call this a promise ring. It symbolizes my commitment to you now and in the future. Where we go, we'll be together. We will never go to bed angry. We will work out our little problems so they won't become big ones.

"We'll continue to talk every day, about anything that affects our lives. Work, family, anything. I just want to hear from you. I can't stand the thought of missing out on something important in your life."

The lump in his throat threatened to choke Ricky. The look on Darwin's face told him the entire story. He'd literally been handed a life on a silver platter, but he knew it would mean work for both of them. He held the ring out to Darwin, then gave him his hand. "Would you?"

Darwin smiled and slipped the band onto Ricky's finger. "I will. Today, tomorrow, forever," he swore.

Then they stood and, in front of friends and family, kissed.

Ricky's mind whirled with thoughts. Even with Darwin claiming his mouth, Ricky grinned. He'd gotten everything he'd ever wanted out of life, but next year, it would be Ricky's chance to return the favor.

~~ The End ~~

Also Available

Haven's Creed

An act of violence destroys his family and ends the life he knows. To escape his haunted past, he joins the military, where, as a sniper, he is trained to kill with precision and detachment. When a covert organization offers him a new purpose, he becomes Haven, an operative devoted to protecting the innocent when he can and avenging them when he cannot.

After ten years of battling the evil in the world, the life no longer holds the attraction or meaning it once had, and he's ready to walk away. Then he meets Samuel, a young man forced from the age of twelve to work as a sex slave. If ever a man had a need for Haven, it is this one.

Yet nothing about this growing relationship is one-sided. Sammy gives Haven a stability he's never known, and Haven becomes the rock upon which Sammy knows he can depend.

When Sammy reveals something about the enemy Haven has been hunting for months, Sammy fears it will destroy what they've built and he'll lose his home in Haven's heart.

500 Miles

Mark loves Jase, but will that be enough to bring Jase back from the brink after a devastating tragedy?

Since he was fourteen, Mark knew he loved Jase, his brother Eric's best friend. As Jase and Eric leave for the Army, Jase leaves Mark something to hold onto, but when the two men are shipped to

Kuwait, things change when Jase tells Mark he's met someone. Confused and hurt, Mark is left to wonder what happened. Eric returns, but with devastating news - and needing Mark's help. Can Mark help the man who broke his heart? Or will he let Jase push him away - for the second time?

Someone to Keep Me_A Collars and Cuffs Novel (with K.C. Wells)

Eighteen-year-old Scott Keating knows a whole world exists beyond his parents' strict control, but until he gains access to the World Wide Web, he really has no idea what's out there. In a chat room, Scott meets "JeffUK." Jeff loves and understands him, and when he offers to bring Scott to the UK, Scott seizes his chance to escape his humdrum life and see the world. But when his plane touches down and Jeff isn't there, panic sets in.

Collars & Cuffs favorite barman and Dom-in-training, Ben Winters, drops his sister off at the airport and finds a lost, anxious Scott. Hearing Scott's story sets off alarm bells, along with his protective instincts. Taking pity on the naïve boy, Ben offers him a place to crash and invites him to Collars & Cuffs, hoping his bosses will know how to help. Scott dreams of belonging to someone, heart and soul. Ben longs for a sub of his own. And neither man sees what's right under his nose.

Mr. Average

Lucas Manetti has had sex with some very hot men, so why is it he can't get one average man out of his mind?

Lucas doesn't want attachments. He thinks life is much easier that way. Watching the way his mom suffered when his father was dying taught him that. But deep down, Lucas likes the idea of someone taking care of him, of coming home to the same person every night. Yeah, what Lucas really wants is love. So why is he settling for random quick sex in seedy bathrooms? Kyle has been taking care of Lucas's car forever. So for Lucas, it's a logical step to think of Kyle taking care of him. And he has so much that he can offer Kyle---whether Kyle wants it or not. So imagine Lucas's surprise when Kyle isn't particularly enamored of Lucas's 'proposition'. Lucas thought his money would buy him anything. And then he realizes... boy, did he get it wrong. He's so busy reeling from the shock that he almost misses what---or who---has been waiting for him all this time.

Storming Love: Bear & Travis

Is it possible to fall in love from nothing more than a few phone calls and e-mails? Dr. David 'Bear' Berickza thinks so. Despite the distance and limited contact, Bear can only think about Travis Michaels, a fellow veterinarian in the small town of Timber Creek.

When he hears that Timber Creek is directly in the path of Hurricane Lauris, Bear makes a promise. He will be there to help Travis and his daughter, the smart-mouthed Tina, to save the abandoned animals.

The road to hell is paved with good intentions, and when Lauris hits, Bear and Travis find that despite their best efforts, it's going to take more than that to save any lives, including their own.

Lost Time

Alex Jeffers and his best friend, Kurt Danvers, were always inseparable. When you found one, you would inevitably find the other. And Alex dreamed it would always be that way.

Kurt swore that when they went to different colleges, nothing would change. They'd keep in contact and would always be best friends. By the time Alex realizes it, he and Kurt have drifted apart. Years of friendship are just...gone.

Starting a new life is scary, but eventually Alex forges ahead and begins building one he's proud of. While at a dinner meeting with a student's father, Alex panics when he sees Kurt Danvers for the first time in five years. He flees the restaurant, but he can't outrun his past as Kurt finds him and lets Alex know that he's not willing to lose him again.

(Please note: This is a new version of the original story, which was a free read at GoodReads. This story has been professionally edited and expanded by 2,000 words, which includes a new ending.)

Damian's Discipline_A Collars and Cuffs Novel (with K.C. Wells)

The man who pimped Jeff may be in prison, but Jeff is still living the nightmare, selling himself to men and relying on pills to manage. Then he meets Scott, a young American man who could easily have been where Jeff is now. Scott's friends extend a helping hand to Jeff, and he grabs it.

Leo and Thomas bring Jeff to stay with Dom Damian Barnett until they can find him someplace more long-term. Still grieving from losing his sub to cancer two years before, Damian agrees to help. But when he glimpses the extent of the damage, Damian wants to do more than offer his guestroom. Jeff is not a submissive, but Damian can see he desperately needs structure in his life. It's up to Damian to find an answer.

He never expects that what he discovers will change both their lives.

Protector of the Alpha

Adopted at an early age by a wealthy family, Jake Davis has always seemed to have an easy life. Even in college he was blessed with good grades and an apparently clear path to a pro football career. Good thing his best friend keeps hanging around to keep his head from getting too swollen.

Zakiya Incekara has always been...odd. Being fluent in six languages and having a flair for international cooking should open the world to him, but those skills leave him isolated.

When Jake sees Zak for the first time, with water beading down his slender form, something inside him shifts, and it hungers for Zak. To have him. To claim him. And Jake knows that whatever it is, it won't be denied.

When they are approached by a man who claims knowledge of a secret past they share, Jake and Zak are thrust into a world they would never have believed existed. The forests of Alaska might seem an odd place to find your destiny, but these men will meet the challenges head on, as they learn that sometimes you have to make sacrifices to be Protector of the Alpha.

Scent of the Heart

Casey Scott grew up being told he'd never amount to anything, and despite the unwavering love and support from his best friend, Jake, the idea sticks in the back of Casey's mind. When he discovers he has a unique destiny in an enclave where shifters and humans live together, he seizes the chance, wanting for once in his life to be someone special.

Tsvetok Yerokhin lost his parents to the evil ruler of the enclave when he was a boy. The responsibilities of raising his two younger brothers nearly overwhelmed him and self-doubt took over. When the new Alpha and his Protector arrive in time to save his life, Sev is grateful, but he's even more shocked when he scents his mate with them.

Casey isn't prepared for the feelings that sweep over him when he meets Sev, but he refuses to act on them because he's straight. Still, there is something so alluring about Sev that Casey can't help being drawn to him.

As the two explore the edges of their new discovery, an evil returns, determined to control the enclave or destroy it. The Alpha and Protector are powerless to stop it, but Casey holds the key to victory. If he can discover what it is, he has a chance to save them all. To be the hero.

Unfortunately, the hero has to be willing to make the ultimate sacrifice, and for Casey that means losing his heart.

Dom of Ages:_A Collars and Cuffs Novel (with K.C. Wells)

Eli may only be thirty, but he has had enough of pretend submissives. When he spies Jarod in a BDSM club, everything about the man screams submission. So what if Jarod is probably twenty years older than Eli. What does age matter, anyway? All he can see is what he's always wanted—a sub who wants to serve.

Jarod spent twenty-four years with his Master before Fate took him. Four years on, Jarod is still lost, so when a young Dom takes charge, Jarod rolls with it and finds himself serving again. But he keeps waiting for the other shoe to drop. Because there's going to come a point when Eli realizes he's a laughingstock in the club. Who would want to be seen with a fifty-year-old sub?

After several missteps, Eli realizes that in order to find happiness, they will need friends who will understand. At a friend's insistence, he visits Collars & Cuffs, where they are met with open arms. As they settle in to their new life, Eli begins to see things differently and he dares to think he can have it all. Until a phone call threatens to take it all away....

ABOUT THE AUTHOR

Parker Williams believes that true love exists, but it always comes with a price. No happily ever after can ever be had without work, sweat, and tears that come with melding lives together.

Living in Milwaukee, Wisconsin, Parker held his job for nearly 28 years before he decided to retire and try new things. He enjoys his new life as a stay-at-home author and also working on Pride-Promotions, an LGBT author promotion service.

Connect with Parker on:

Twitter: @ParkerWAuthor

Facebook:
https://www.facebook.com/parker.williams.75641

Or you can visit his website: ParkerWilliamsAuthor.com

www.ingramcontent.com/pod-product-compliance
Lightning Source LLC
Chambersburg PA
CBHW030257130626
46549CB00002B/566